Sui
Cruise S
Mysteries Series
Book 8

MW01136522

Hope Callaghan

hopecallaghan.com
***

Visit my website for new releases and special offers:
hopecallaghan.com

Thank you, Peggy H., Jean P., Cindi G., Wanda D. and Barbara W. for taking the time to preview *Suite Revenge,* for the extra sets of eyes and for catching all my mistakes.

A special thanks to my reader review team: Alice, Amary, Barbara, Becky, Becky B, Brinda, Cassie, Christina, Debbie, Denota, Devan, Francine, Grace, Jan, Jo-Ann, Joeline, Joyce, Jean K., Jean M., Kathy, Lynne, Megan, Melda, Kat, Linda, Lynne, Pat, Patsy, Paula, Renate, Rita, Rita P, Shelba, Tamara and Vicki

i

Table of Contents

Chapter 1 2

Chapter 2.. 19

Chapter 3... 37

Chapter 4..54

Chapter 5..68

Chapter 6... 79

Chapter 7..92

Chapter 8....................................... 107

Chapter 9.......................................121

Chapter 10 139

Chapter 11......................................150

Chapter 12 162

Chapter 13 183

Chapter 14 199

Chapter 15 215

Chapter 16 236

Chapter 17...................................... 252

Chapter 18 262

Chapter 19 279

Chapter 20......................................289

Get Free Books and More! 292

Meet The Author 293

Chicken Pot Pie Recipe............................... 294

"And there were in the same country shepherds abiding in the field, keeping watch over their flock by night.

And, lo, the angel of the Lord came upon them, and the glory of the Lord shone round about them: and they were sore afraid.

And the angel said unto them, Fear not: for, behold, I bring you good tidings of great joy, which shall be to all people. For unto you is born this day in the city of David a Saviour, which is Christ the Lord.

And this shall be a sign unto you; Ye shall find the babe wrapped in swaddling clothes, lying in a manger.

And suddenly there was with the angel a multitude of the heavenly host praising God, and saying, Glory to God in the highest, and on earth peace, good will toward men. Luke 2: 8-14 (KJV)

Chapter 1

Millie Sanders tugged her bursting-at-the-seams suitcase off the curb and hurried across the street. She stopped abruptly when she reached the other side. Her heart skipped a beat as she caught a glimpse of Siren of the Seas, her second home.

It seemed like forever since she'd taken her mandatory break as assistant cruise director on board Siren of the Seas and traveled home to Michigan to visit family and friends.

Millie had planned to return to work on Siren of the Seas a couple months back, but there had been a mix-up in her paperwork and the corporate office had assigned her to Baroness of

2

the Seas instead. Baroness, one of Majestic Cruise Lines newer ships, would have been perfect except for the fact that her heart, and Captain Armati was on Siren of the Seas.

The break had been wonderful and given Millie a chance to recharge her batteries and spend precious time with her family. Her daughter, Beth, had surprised her and told her the family planned to join her for a cruise the same week she returned to work on Siren of the Seas. Millie's grandchildren were starting their Christmas break and the timing would work out perfectly.

Millie had flown to Miami a couple days early to wrap up some loose ends and fill out a pile of paperwork the corporate office required before she could start her new contract.

Beth had also told her there was another surprise but Millie had a sneaky suspicion it wasn't a pleasant one. Beth had refused to elaborate and told her mother she would rather tell her in person.

Millie pushed the nagging feeling something unpleasant was about to happen out of her mind and instead thought of her upcoming reunion with her close friends, Annette Delacroix and Cat Wellington, not to mention her boss, Andy Walker.

There was also one very special person Millie couldn't wait to see...Captain Armati.

She hurried through the employee check-in counter where she picked up her new employee identification card. Millie let out the small breath she'd been holding when she spotted the corner emblem indicating the cardholder held a level two security clearance. Level two was below the ship's officers and other high ranking officials, but it still gave her access to many areas of the ship that were restricted.

She picked up the pace as she marched up the steep ramp that led to the ship.

The familiar "ding" of keycards echoed inside the entrance as Millie stopped behind a group of other crewmembers. None of them looked familiar and she knew that, like her, others were coming back on board after a break or were switching from one ship to another.

Millie reached the front of the line and a beaming Suharto, one of the security officers who manned the entrance, smiled broadly. "Miss Millie! You decided to come back!"

Millie slid her keycard in the slot and waited for the familiar *ding*. "Of course, Suharto. You can't get rid of me that easy," she teased as she removed the card from the slot.

She stood off to the side and gazed at the magnificent glass and brass atrium, as if seeing it for the very first time. A towering Christmas tree filled the center of the room. The twinkling red, blue and green lights winked at Millie and the soft strains of *Jingle Bells* filled the air.

The familiar smell of freshly brewed coffee wafted across the room from the beverage bar and Millie closed her eyes, breathing in the aroma.

"It'll all still be here when you open your eyes," a familiar voice whispered in her ear.

Millie opened her eyes and came face-to-face with Andy Walker, Siren of the Seas Cruise Director and Millie's boss. She let go of her suitcase and flung herself at him. "Did you miss me?" she asked as she hugged him tight.

"Of course not," Andy teased. He waited for Millie to release her hold and held her at arm's length. "Your hair looks a little grayer and I see another wrinkle or two but other than that, I'm guessing you enjoyed your time off."

Millie playfully slugged him in the arm. "That's not nice," she shot back, the smile never leaving her face.

"I'm joking," Andy said. "You look great. I'm the one who has more gray hair and extra wrinkles. It's been a nightmare having Zack fill in for you while you were gone." Zack was one of the dancers and a member of the entertainment staff.

"Good. I hope you were miserable." Millie quickly glanced around the atrium. "Is everyone else already on board?"

"If 'everyone else' is Captain Armati, then the answer is 'yes.' He's up in the bridge and nearly driving me nuts calling me on the radio every ten minutes to ask if you've arrived yet."

"He has?" Millie's face turned a hint of pink and she beamed brightly.

"Well, more like every twenty minutes," Andy said as he glanced at his watch. "You have another hour before the first passengers start boarding." He pointed at Millie's large suitcase. "Why don't you go on ahead and drop your suitcase off in your cabin? You should have plenty of time to make a stop by the bridge so the captain will quit calling me."

"I'm still sharing a cabin with Danielle?" Danielle was Danielle Kneldon, another member of the entertainment staff and although her official title wasn't assistant cruise director, she shared many of the same responsibilities as Millie. "Is she here?"

"Yep," Andy said. "She's another one who's been chomping at the bit, anxiously awaiting your arrival."

"It feels good to be loved." Millie reached for the suitcase handle. "I'll report back within the hour." She saluted her boss and then headed to the bank of elevators and the stairs on the other side.

She was tempted to take the elevators, just this once, but her claustrophobia wasn't having it. Her heart began to pound at the thought and she quickly decided to lug her bag down the steps to the crew quarters, which were located on deck one.

When she reached the employee corridor, nicknamed I-95 by the ship's crew, she passed several familiar faces. Some she knew by name and they welcomed her back on board the ship.

A red and white striped candy cane sticker was stuck to the front of her cabin door with the words 'Welcome Home' neatly written on the front.

Millie smiled as she pulled the lanyard from around her neck and slipped the keycard into the slot, waiting for the familiar beep.

She pushed the door open and dragged her suitcase across the threshold before maneuvering the bulky bag out of the doorway. She waited for the door to close before opening one of the closet doors, the one she'd previously used. It was empty.

After quickly unpacking her suitcase and hanging her work uniforms on the hangers, she slid the empty suitcase to the far corner of the closet.

Millie placed her makeup bag in the bathroom and changed into her work uniform. After changing into her uniform and freshening up, Millie hurried from the cabin, down the corridor and up the stairs to deck ten, where the captain's bridge was located.

She strode to the door, lifted her lanyard to use her keycard and then stopped. She'd always let herself into the bridge, but that had been before.

The door abruptly swung open and Antonio Vitale, the ship's staff captain, nearly plowed her over.

"Millie." He jumped back. "It's so nice to see your lovely face," he said, his thick Italian accent unmistakable. "We've missed you."

"I've missed you too. I thought I would pop in to say hello to the captain."

Captain Vitale nodded. "I was getting ready to grab a bite to eat. The captain and Scout are in the bridge."

Scout was Captain Armati's teacup Yorkshire pup. The dog and Millie spent a lot of time together during her working hours when she took Scout out several times a week to visit with ship's guests, including the junior passengers. They also liked to spend time at Ocean Oasis, a special place on board the ship Captain Armati had built for Scout and Millie.

Millie waited for the door to shut behind Captain Vitale before she tiptoed up the steps and into the bridge. Captain Armati stood front and center, holding a pair of binoculars to his eyes.

Scout spotted Millie first as he let out a small yip and scampered across the floor. He pounced on her shoe, pawed at her leg and let out a low whine.

Millie picked up the pint-size fur ball and held him close. Scout promptly licked her face, attempted to bite her necklace and then head butted her chin.

He wiggled and squirmed until she finally set him back on the floor where he circled her legs. She looked up and her eyes locked with Captain Armati's eyes.

Millie's breath caught and she let out a small squeak, which was supposed to be 'hello' but didn't quite make it.

"Millie." A wave of warmth washed over Millie's body as her name rolled off the captain's tongue.

"H-hello Captain Armati."

"Nic," he corrected as he set the binoculars on top of the computer console and crossed the room.

Millie stood. "Nic," she whispered as he got close.

"I've missed you," he said, right before he leaned down and softly kissed her lips.

Millie placed both hands on the captain's chest. He took it as an invitation and drew her closer as the kiss deepened.

The kiss...his closeness, was Millie's undoing and she lost all sense of time as they stood locked in a flame-worthy embrace.

Scout, not happy at being ignored, began barking and raced over the top of their feet. They reluctantly took a step back and Millie fought to steady her breathing. She placed a hand over her heart. "I-I'm sorry." She blurted out the first thing that came to mind.

"I'm not." Captain Armati's eyes smoldered. "I was just getting started."

Millie's heart flip-flopped and she began to stutter again. "W-well."

Captain Armati touched her arm. "Let's just say it's a good thing Scout is here to chaperone."

Before she could answer, the doorknob rattled and Donovan Sweeney, the ship's purser, stepped inside.

He took one look at Millie's face and stopped in his tracks. "I hope I'm not interrupting."

Millie cleared her throat, hoping Donovan hadn't noticed the flushed look on her face. "I was just leaving," she said.

Donovan strode across the room to give Millie a quick hug. "We've missed you 'round here. It's been quiet and boring. We haven't had a single man overboard nor stumbled upon a single dead body."

"I'll see if I can change that," Millie quipped as she returned the hug. "It's good to be home."

She smiled. "I better get going." Millie patted Scout's head and made a hasty retreat.

Millie's next stop was Waves, the ship's buffet area, where she planned to grab a bite to eat but quickly realized it wasn't open yet.

There was also a deli station and pizza station, across from the buffet. Millie wandered over to study the menus. One of the crew turned and although he looked familiar, Millie couldn't quite place the name.

"Welcome back Miss Millie. We're getting ready for the lunch crowd. Can I get something for you?"

Millie ordered a turkey Reuben with extra sauerkraut and Thousand Island dressing. She grabbed a bag of corn chips from the chip display rack and placed them on the side of her plate, next to the sandwich before thanking the crew and wandering to a nearby table.

It was good to be back, to be home. She gobbled her food and sipped her watered down iced tea before placing her dirty dishes in the bin near the door and heading down to deck five.

Andy, who was already there, glanced at his watch. "Two minutes to spare," he teased.

"Right on time," Millie argued. "Have I ever been late? Don't answer that!"

Suharto gave Andy two thumbs up, his signal the passengers were starting up the ramp.

"It's show time folks," Andy bellowed to the staff and crew inside the atrium.

Millie fixed a smile on her face and kept it there as the first wave of passengers, the diamond level guests, arrived. Several of them were regulars, and Andy and Millie greeted many of them by name.

Next in line were platinum guests. She even remembered several of their names. Between lulls, Millie managed to tell Andy her children would be joining them, that they had surprised her with the news of booking a cruise while she'd been on leave. She was excited to see them again and have them meet the Siren of the Seas crew.

The crowds finally started to thin and Millie caught a glimpse of Beth's face. David, Beth's husband, was beside her. Behind them were

Noah and Bella, Millie's grandchildren. They darted across the floor when they spotted their 'Nana.'

"Nana!" Bella tugged on the edge of her grandmother's jacket. "Mommy said we might get to see Santa Claus while we're here!"

Millie hugged each of them. "Wouldn't that be fun?" She wasn't sure if "Santa Claus" was onboard, but Andy knew as he knelt down in front of the children. "I heard that he'll be here later tonight." Andy pointed toward the Christmas tree. "Right over there so be sure to come down here after dinner."

"Can we?" Noah's bright blue eyes grew serious.

"Of course," Beth said as she patted her son's shoulder.

"I would love to bring them down for a visit." Millie reached for Bella's hand. "But first you'll need to find your cabin and get settled in."

"Why don't you give them a quick tour of the ship and show them to their cabins?" Andy said.

"Thanks Andy. I'll be back in a minute." Millie waved her hand. "Follow me."

She spun on her heel and nearly collided with her ex-husband, Roger Sanders.

Chapter 2

Millie's mouth dropped open as she stared at her ex-husband in disbelief. She shifted her gaze. Roger's girlfriend, Delilah Osborne, was right behind him.

"Millie, you look surprised to see me." Roger grinned evilly.

Beth rushed forward. "I'm sorry Mom. I-I didn't know how to tell you Dad and Delilah booked this cruise, as well."

More than anything, Millie wished the floor would open up and swallow her. She hadn't seen her ex since the day she'd signed the divorce papers, not long after Roger had come home from work and told her he was leaving her for one of his clients, who also happened to be a friend of Millie's...Delilah.

Delilah eased past Roger. She waved a large sparkling diamond ring in front of Millie's face. "Dear Millie. You look wonderful. Why I can hardly see those deep wrinkles on your face what with all the makeup you're wearing, or is it tanned skin from overexposure to the sun?" Delilah squinted her eyes and leaned forward to examine Millie up close.

Millie, still in a state of shock, stared, unable to comprehend the fact two people she wished she never had to face again were standing in front of her. Not only that, they were on Siren of the Seas...*her* ship, *her* home.

"Are you going to show us to our cabin too?" Delilah handed her carry-on bag to Millie. "We're in an owner's suite. Before you show us to our suite, I'd like to stop by the salon to make an appointment to have my hair done before the wedding."

The word wedding buzzed in Millie's ear. She felt two things at once, an overwhelming urge to throw up followed by the urge to whack Delilah Osborne over the head with her bag. Instead, she tightened her grip on the bag and clenched her teeth.

"I'll take care of them." Danielle materialized out of nowhere. She took Delilah's bag from Millie and grasped Delilah under the arm. "Right this way." Danielle didn't wait for a reply as she steered the woman toward the nearest bank of elevators.

Roger trailed behind like a puppy dog.

Beth slipped her hand into her mother's hand. "Mom. I am so sorry. I didn't know how to tell you. I was going to tell you when we talked last week, but you were so excited to be coming back to Siren of the Seas and Captain Armati, I chickened out." Beth babbled on. "I tried to give Dad and Delilah the slip so I could warn you before they boarded but they stuck by us like glue."

The sensation of disbelief began to fade, replaced by a rage Millie hadn't felt since the night she built a bonfire in her backyard and torched Roger's belongings. "I forgive you, Beth, but as you can imagine, I'm very upset right now."

"There's one more thing," Beth lowered her voice. "Dad and Delilah are getting married on board the ship tomorrow, by the captain. They asked Linda, Delilah's daughter, to stand up with them. They asked me but I told them I couldn't."

"Is there any more good news?" Millie groaned.

"I think that about sums it up, other than the fact you're going to be stuck with them for a week." Beth moved away from her husband and children. "There are a few others coming on board...Delilah's sister and brother-in-law along with Delilah's daughter and son-in-law and another couple. I'll try to give you a heads up so you can keep an eye out for them."

Andy, who had been hovering nearby, stepped close. "You go ahead Millie. Show Beth and her family to their cabins. I'll cover here. I'm sure Danielle will come back to help."

Millie nodded, relieved she would have a few moments to pull herself together and try to wrap her head around what had just happened. She shifted into assistant cruise director mode as she escorted her family on a brief tour of the ship.

A fresh wave of determination washed over Millie. Roger had done this on purpose, to shove his soon-to-be wife and her family in Millie's face. It wasn't bad enough he'd cheated on her and walked out after 38 years of marriage, but now he was rubbing it in.

The old Millie would've crawled into bed and stayed there for a week, until they'd disembarked the ship, but not now. The new Millie was strong, stronger than she'd ever been and with each step Millie took, she became more determined to prove to Roger, to Delilah, that she was not going to be intimidated by them, by any of them.

Millie finished giving them a ship tour and led them to their cabin where she excused herself and made her way back to Andy.

Andy smiled as Millie marched across the atrium and resumed her position near the gangway. "Ah. I see the Millie I know and love, the one with more spunk than a hundred Delilahs, has returned."

"They're going to regret ever setting foot on board my ship," Millie vowed.

Andy chuckled. "I almost feel sorry for them. Almost."

A group of passengers descended on them and Millie pushed the thoughts of Delilah and Roger to the back of her mind. She would deal with it later. Right now, she had a job to do.

Millie smiled as she greeted a couple of "regulars" she'd come to know over the past year.

They welcomed Millie back on board and told her they'd missed her while she was gone. "It's good to be back." *Despite Roger and Delilah's unexpected arrival.*

The rest of the afternoon flew by. After the last passenger boarded and the crew removed the gangway, Millie headed to the lido deck to check on the Sail Away Party. She waved to Felix, one of the dancers in charge of the line dancing. He winked and blew Millie a 'welcome back' kiss. She shook her head before returning the gesture.

Her steps were light as she made her rounds, greeting the other crew, her friends. Roger was on her turf now. He had made an unwise decision to board her ship and taunt her with his upcoming nuptials.

She vowed to avoid him and his entourage at all costs. The last thing she needed was drama. She'd had enough drama to last a lifetime.

Millie swung by Ocean Treasures Gift Shop where her friend, Cat, worked. There were only a couple shoppers milling about since it was nearing the dinner hour. She stepped inside and made a beeline to the back where Cat was chatting with a passenger.

Cat smiled when she caught Millie's eye and Millie stood off to the side to wait until the customer paid for their purchases and exited the store.

"Ohhh! I've missed you, my friend!" Cat darted around the side of the cash register and hugged Millie. "This joint has been as dull as a butter knife since you left. Annette and I were on the verge of plotting a crisis just to liven the place up."

Millie hugged Cat and took a step back. "I missed you too. There's something different. You changed your hair." Cat's signature jet-black beehive hairdo was gone. In its place was a glossy coat of smooth black hair. The tips touched the top of her shoulders.

Cat smoothed her hair. "I'm trying something new. Joe talked me into it."

"Joe?" Millie frowned. "Who's Joe?"

"Doctor Gundervan. You know. Joe Gundervan."

"Ah." Millie lifted a brow. "That Joe. It must be serious if he's talking you into changing your hairstyle."

"Nah!" Cat waved a dismissive hand. "We've gone out on a couple dates since you left and now that I'm finally able to leave the ship without freaking out." She stopped abruptly. "Okay. Whom am I kidding? Yes, we're dating."

Millie grinned. "That's wonderful, Cat. I'm so happy for you."

Cat had been through a lot since Millie had met her. Cat's ex-husband, a convicted felon, had escaped from prison, tracked her down, kidnapped her and almost killed her. Thankfully, he was back behind bars. The experience had been so traumatic; Cat had refused to leave the safety of the cruise ship.

Millie and their friend, Annette, had become so desperate they'd hired a psychologist on the island of St. Thomas to meet with Cat and work with her. "How is Doctor Johansen? Are you still seeing her?"

"Yep." Cat nodded. "Not for much longer, though. I'm doing so much better now, thanks to you and Annette. I even went shopping in Miami last week while we were in port."

"That's great news!" Several more shoppers wandered into the store. Millie said her good-byes and promised to catch up with her friend soon.

She exited the store and headed toward the galley where her friend Annette worked. When Millie reached the galley, she peeked through the window and quickly changed her mind. The place was a beehive of activity as the galley crew rushed around the kitchen.

Millie glanced at her watch. They were right in the middle of the first and second seating for dinner.

Vowing to return later, Millie stepped away from the galley door and headed to Andy's office to check on tomorrow's schedule. She fleetingly wondered if Roger and his soon-to-be-new family would be in the audience.

Get a grip! There's nothing you can do...not for the next seven days until they get off the ship.

Millie turned the corner and started down the steps leading to the stage and the back where Andy's office was located.

"Wait!"

Millie spun around and caught a glimpse of Danielle hurrying to catch up with her. "I've been looking all over for you," the young woman said when she caught up with Millie. "You sure know how to liven things up around here."

"I assume you're talking about my ex and his entourage."

Danielle rolled her eyes. "That woman, Delilah what's-her-name is a witch with a capital 'W.' I almost feel sorry for your ex."

"Don't," Millie said. "They deserve each other." She began walking and Danielle fell into step.

"Did you catch the part where Nic...Captain Armati is marrying them on board the ship? Can you believe the nerve of your ex?" Millie could feel her blood beginning to boil again.

"You would've laughed if you'd seen them together," Danielle said. "She was bossing him around as if he was some sort of servant." She lifted her voice an octave. "Roger! Turn the air conditioning down. It's too hot in here. This bed is lumpy. You call this tiny space a bathroom? How much did they charge us for this dump?"

Millie chuckled at Danielle's imitation of Delilah. "That makes me feel a little better."

"If I were him, I'd pitch the witch overboard." Danielle laughed. "Get it? Pitch the witch? It has a nice ring to it."

Millie followed Danielle up the side steps and their heels echoed on the stage floor as they hurried to the back. "Another couple stopped by their suite as I was leaving. The woman looked a lot like Delilah so I'm guessing they're related."

"It was probably Delilah's sister," Millie said. "They're here to help celebrate the joyous nuptials."

Danielle brushed her hands together. "I say good riddance. You're lucky. I'd be counting my blessings every day to be rid of that circus."

A dim light shone from the bottom of Andy's door. Millie tapped lightly, turned the knob and eased the door open.

Andy was sitting at the conference table, his head down as he studied a clipboard in front of him. He shifted his gaze and looked up. "Right on time, gals. I take it you both survived your run-in with Millie's ex?"

"Whew!" Danielle yanked out a chair and plopped down next to her boss. "What a trip. I was telling Millie she should count her blessings."

Andy tapped the tip of his pen on the paper in front of him. "My suggestion is to avoid them as much as possible."

"You don't have to tell me," Millie mumbled. She changed the subject and pointed at the papers. "Are you working on tomorrow's schedule?"

"Yep." Andy slid a sheet to Millie and another to Danielle. "It's so nice to have my whole crew back on board. I have a couple new activities I've been tossing around and decided now would be the perfect time to give them a go."

Millie slipped her reading glasses on and studied her schedule for the following day. She scanned the list, which started with Sunrise

Stride. She noticed she was also in charge of two trivia games as well as co-hosting the cruise's first round of bingo.

There was also wine tasting with the ship's sommelier, Pierre LeBlanc. When she got to the first activity after her lunch break, she paused. "What is Cruise Clue?"

"I'm glad you asked," Andy said as he stuck his hand under his clipboard and pulled out a small stack of papers. "It's a new adult murder mystery/crime-themed activity."

Danielle snorted. "That's right up Millie's alley."

Millie shot Danielle a death look and reached for the stack of papers. "This is part of it?"

"Those are the clues," Andy nodded. "I came up with the first set while you were gone. I was thinking if it went well, I'd let you run with it and you come up with the mystery and clues."

Millie glanced at the paper on top. It was intriguing...a mystery game on board the ship.

"I put together a list of instructions. Some of the entertainment staff and I practiced with a mock game to try to work out the kinks. I think it's going to be one of our most popular activities once we get it up and running."

"What about me?" Danielle asked. "Do I get to host any cool new activities?"

"Yep." Andy nodded as he reached for another sheet and slid it to Danielle. "I've put you in charge of our new dating game event. Remember the 60's show 'The Dating Game' where the contestant asked questions of prospective dates, who were hidden behind a wall and the contestant chose the winner based on the answers?"

Danielle frowned. "No. That was decades before I was even born!"

Millie burst out laughing. Danielle hated hosting the "Mix and Mingle" singles parties. This was the icing on the cake.

"It's not funny." Danielle shot Millie a dark look.

"It'll be fun. You need to give it a chance, Danielle," Andy said. He went over a few new changes he'd implemented in Millie's absence and then stood. "It's time for me to have a pre-show pep talk with the dancers, unless, of course, you have any questions?"

"I don't." Millie stood and Andy lifted his hand. "Don't forget about the visit with Santa Claus later this evening."

"Thanks for the reminder." Millie had almost forgotten. Noah and Bella would be deeply disappointed if they missed a visit with Santa.

Danielle and Millie wandered out of Andy's office. "How come you always get the good stuff?" Danielle grumbled when they were out of earshot.

"Tell you what, you try your dating game show tomorrow and I'll host the mystery game and then next week, if you want, we'll switch to make it fair."

The girls parted ways with Danielle taking her break and Millie heading back to the cabin to drop off the schedules and freshen up for the evening show. She wandered down the corridor to her cabin. As she got closer, she noticed a woman dressed to the nines in high heels and a skin-tight shimmering cocktail party dress, lounging outside her door. It was Delilah Osborne.

Chapter 3

Millie fleetingly contemplated turning around and heading in the opposite direction, but curiosity got the better of her. She wondered why on earth Delilah was outside her cabin door. She also wondered how the woman had managed to gain access to a "crew only" area.

"Hello," Millie said coolly as she approached her cabin door.

Delilah twisted her sparkly stiletto heel and attempted to peer down at Millie despite the fact Delilah was a good three inches shorter than her fiancé's ex-wife was.

She lifted her hand and flashed her diamond ring in front of Millie's eyes. "I cannot believe someone lives in these squalid conditions. Is there running water in this part of the ship?"

The palm of Millie's hand began to itch and the urge to slap the smug expression off Delilah's face was overwhelming. Instead, she clenched her fist and dug her fingernails into the palms of her hands. "This area is off limits to *guests*. How did you get down here?"

"A nice uniformed man escorted me. I think his name was Simon or something," Delilah answered. "He was a bit reluctant until I stuck a twenty-dollar bill in his hand. Twenty dollars must be a lot of money for overworked servants like yourself."

Millie lunged forward. Visions of wrapping her hands around Delilah's neck and strangling her filled her head.

Delilah, noting the look in Millie's eyes, took a tentative step back. "This isn't a social call."

"You could've fooled me."

Delilah ignored the sarcastic reply. "The reason I'm here is to ask if you'd be interested in selling your home in Grand Rapids. It's obvious you're not using it anymore. The dump isn't worth much in its current condition. I was thinking if you let Roger and me purchase it from you, we could tear it down and build a new home. The value, of course, is in the land."

Millie's Michigan home was located on the shores of Reeds Lake, one of the most prestigious lakes in the area. A large picture window boasted a magnificent view of the lake. Although the home, built in the late 1980's, was dated, she and Roger had taken good care of the home. It needed some cosmetic updates but other than that, was in tiptop shape.

"Roger put you up to this?" Millie gritted through clenched teeth.

"No. He told me to let it go but I can't. My – our - condo is cramped and developers are building a high rise unit that will eventually block my view of Lake Michigan. I simply can't stay there without a view," Delilah rattled on. "Another reason is my daughter may be moving in with us soon and we need more room. What would you be willing to sell the house for?" She stared at Millie expectantly.

"My home is not for sale," Millie said. "Not now. Not later. Not ever, at least not for you." Her level of anger grew at the thought of Delilah razing her home and building a brand new one in its place.

"Three hundred fifty grand," Delilah countered.

"No."

"Three seventy five."

"NO!"

"Four hundred thousand dollars. That's my final offer," Delilah said.

"No. No. No. Never!" Millie could hear her own voice as she screeched at Delilah. A cluster of the ship's crew passing by them gave the women an odd stare.

One of them stopped. "Is everything okay Miss Millie?"

"Yes. Thank you Tariq." Millie forced a smile. "Ms. Osborne was leaving." She clamped a hand around Delilah's arm and propelled her down the hall.

"Let go of me." Delilah hissed as she stumbled forward on her high heels, attempting to keep up with Millie's fast clip. "You're making a scene."

"You made a scene when you decided to show up on my doorstep," Millie said.

Delilah whined the entire way but Millie refused to release her grip. She stopped in front of the door that led to the passenger area and reached for the handle. "Do not ever show your face down here again or you'll be sorry." She yanked the door open and glared at Delilah.

"No wonder Roger left you. What a horrid woman." Delilah stepped over the threshold and shot Millie a dirty look before stomping up the steps.

"Good riddance." Millie slammed the door and started down the hall.

The door suddenly swung open. Millie spun around, certain it was Delilah but it was Annette hurrying toward her.

"Whew! What was that all about? I could hear you and the blonde woman yelling from two decks up."

"My ex-husband's soon-to-be-wife," Millie said.

Annette nodded. "Ahh... So you decided to bring them back with you?"

"They followed me," Millie groaned. While they walked, Millie explained to Annette what had transpired from the moment Roger and Delilah boarded the ship and finished with a recap of the heated exchange she'd had with Delilah.

"Captain Armati agreed to marry them?" Annette asked.

"Does he have a choice?" They reached Millie's cabin and she leaned her forehead against the door. "Am I a terrible person if I said I wished she...they were dead?"

"No and I can't say as I blame you. I ran into Danielle and she told me briefly about the woman." Annette shook her head. "It sounds as if the two of them deserve each other. I'm on break. Do you have time to grab a bite to eat and catch up?"

"Sure." Millie nodded. "I need to drop off the work schedules for tomorrow." She darted inside her cabin, dropped the sheets on the desk and hurried out to where Annette was waiting in the hall.

While they ate, Annette entertained Millie with stories of what she had missed while she was on leave. It was a welcome diversion from dwelling on Roger and Delilah, and by the time she finished eating, Millie felt much better.

Annette gave her some sound advice, to avoid Delilah and her ex at all costs. She reminded Millie they would be gone before she knew it.

Millie glanced at her watch. "I need to go get my grandchildren. They want to visit Santa down in the atrium." She left Annette in the hall outside the galley before hurrying to her daughter's cabin where she found the children bouncing off the walls.

Millie smiled at her granddaughter, dressed in a bright red velvet dress. Beth had curled her hair into what she fondly called "Shirley Temple" curls and added a matching velvet headband to hold the curls in place.

"You look beautiful." Millie hugged Bella.

"What about me Nana?" Millie turned to Noah, dressed in a pair of crisp navy blue dress slacks, a button down shirt and a festive green and red striped Christmas tie.

Millie tugged on the tip of Noah's tie. "My goodness, you look so handsome. I think I need

44

to have my picture taken with both of you." She dropped to her knees. Noah stood on one side while Bella stood on the other. Beth grabbed her cell phone, switched it to camera mode and snapped a picture.

Millie gave them both a quick hug and sprang to her feet. "Shall we go find Santa now?" She winked at her daughter and they followed Beth to the door. "Thanks for taking them Mom."

"Of course dear," Millie said. "I wouldn't miss this for the world."

The children chattered excitedly as they made their way to the atrium and over to the Christmas tree. There were a dozen other children ahead of them, all dressed in Christmas attire and anxiously awaiting their turn to visit with the jolly old elf.

When they reached the front of the line, Bella went first and she immediately hopped onto Santa's lap. Santa put a light hand around her shoulder and leaned in to listen as she whispered in his ear.

"Ho, ho. We'll see what we can do," Santa said as his "belly" jiggled and he helped her down.

Noah and Bella traded places and Bella came back to stand next to her grandmother. She tugged on Millie's hand and Millie leaned down. "Nana, he talks funny," she whispered in her grandmother's ear.

"He does?" Millie and Bella took a step closer as Noah and Santa chatted. She could just make out what was being said and a distinct British accent with the word "lift" in place of "elevator." The jolly old elf was none other than Andy. He caught Millie's eye and winked as Noah slid off his knee.

Millie winked back as she reached for Noah's hand and they headed toward a brightly decorated Christmas table for a glass of cold milk and a frosted sugar cookie coated with a thick layer of red sprinkles.

The worker behind the table was dressed in elf attire, complete with a satin green jacket that sported bright red buttons and white faux fur trim. A thick red belt circled his waist. The elf wore striped knee socks and a green elf hat and looked vaguely familiar. He handed each of the children a Christmas gift bag.

Millie leaned across the table. "Brody?"

The elf's eyes narrowed. "Yeah, it's me. I'm guarding Santa."

"What..." A slow smile crept across Millie's face and she reached for her cell phone, switched it to camera and took a picture of the frowning elf. "You look adorable."

The elf groaned. "Great. Instead of attracting chicks, I'm attracting kids and grandmas."

Millie's chuckle turned into a laugh. She laughed so hard, tears rolled down her cheeks. "I love it."

"I thought elves were s'posed to be little, like me." Bella wrinkled her nose and frowned at the elf.

Noah opened up his goodie bag, peeked inside the bag and handed it to Millie so he could eat his cookie. "Nana, Santa said we should take the lift. What is a lift?" he asked.

"The elevator," Millie explained. "Santa has spent too much time in Europe, I'm afraid. You know Nana does not like elevators so we'll stick to the stairs."

Millie opened the bag of goodies. Inside was a packet of holiday stickers, a candy cane, a Christmas coloring book and a small box of crayons.

After they finished their sweet treat, Millie took the children back to their cabin and chatted with her daughter and David. "We had a wonderful time. They visited with Santa, ate a Christmas cookie and each of them got a small gift bag."

"Santa talks funny," Bella said. "But I think he's just trying to disguise his voice."

Millie chuckled. "You could be right, Bella. Santa is disguising his voice."

She hugged her daughter and grandchildren good-bye before heading downstairs to peek in on the second "Welcome Aboard" show and then headed to the comedy show.

The early "family friendly" comedy show, held in the Paradise Lounge, was packed. She continued toward the piano bar, which was just warming up, made a quick pass through the casino and ended her tour on the sports deck. It was empty except for a small line of passengers waiting their turn to climb the rock wall.

A cool breeze blew through the aft, the back of the ship, and Millie slipped over to the railing. She propped her elbows on the top of the rail, closed her eyes and breathed the ocean air. She could feel her muscles relax and the tension leave her body.

She stood silently at the rail as the soft strains of steel drums drifted up from the lido deck.

Millie squinted her eyes to check her watch. Although it was late and she was exhausted, she had one more stop to make. She needed to check in with Robert, the bartender in charge of the Tahitian Nights dance club.

The place was packed and the dance floor thumped as the beat of the music pulsated. Millie shouted in an attempt to be heard over the loud music as she asked Robert if he needed anything. Robert gave Millie a thumbs up everything was okay.

Brody, no longer dressed like an oversized elf, stood guard near the entrance. He grinned at Millie before giving her a mock salute. "Miss Millie. We've missed you 'round here. We were beginning to wonder if you were coming back."

"Thanks. I've missed you, too and I'm glad to be back. What happened to the elf costume?" she teased.

"Santa had to head back to the North Pole." Brody changed the subject. "While you were gone, Patterson promoted me to head of night security."

Millie smiled as she remembered the time Andy had tased Brody during a safety demonstration and how Brody had turned the tables as he yanked the Taser out of Andy's hand and zapped him. "Way to go, Brody! You deserve it."

Millie said her good-byes and headed down to her empty cabin where she brushed her teeth, washed her face and changed into her pajamas before crawling into bed.

It had been an eventful day. Tomorrow promised to be even more eventful with Roger and Delilah's 'blissful nuptials.'

Millie and Beth had planned a fun day for the entire family when the ship docked in St. Croix and included a snorkeling excursion at Buck Island. Captain Armati, Nic, had also invited

Millie's family to join him for dinner at the captain's table the last night of the cruise.

She drifted off into a dreamless sleep and woke briefly sometime during the night when she heard Danielle sneak in. It would take some getting used to sharing cramped quarters again, but Millie wouldn't have it any other way.

Her alarm woke her early the next morning and she groggily shut it off before crawling out of bed and tiptoeing to the bathroom. She slipped into a pair of gym shorts and t-shirt after brushing her teeth and washing her face. On her way out of the cabin, she grabbed her lanyard.

Dave Patterson, Siren of the Seas' head of security was coming toward her, a somber expression on his face.

"Good morning." Millie tentatively smiled. She hadn't seen Patterson since returning. "Aren't you a ray of sunshine at this early hour," she joked.

"I'm sorry Millie. I'd hoped to welcome you back on board the ship under more pleasant circumstances," Dave said.

"What do you mean more pleasant circumstances?" Millie's smile vanished.

"Delilah Osborne, your husband's fiancée, was found dead inside her cabin last night."

Chapter 4

Millie's jaw dropped as she stared at Patterson in disbelief. "Dead?"

"Ms. Osborne expired late last night. She suffered a severe allergic reaction." Dave Patterson shifted to the side and lowered his voice. "From what I've been told, your ex-husband and Ms. Osborne gave chef cards to the ship's staff and crew to inform them of her severe nut allergy. After returning to their room late last night, they ordered room service and again, reminded the staff on the phone of Ms. Osborne's allergies."

Patterson continued. "Mr. Sanders ran upstairs to grab some drinks after realizing they forgot to order sodas and when he returned, he found Ms. Osborne lying on the bed, a half-eaten cream puff in one hand and clutching her throat with the other."

"That's terrible," Millie said. "They think someone intentionally delivered food that contained nuts?"

"I'm afraid so and Mr. Sanders believes that person is you."

"Me?" Millie squeaked. "That's absurd. I can't stand the woman, but what reason would I have to do her in?"

"Other than she was going to marry your ex-husband today and Mr. Sanders said Ms. Osborne and you got into a heated argument yesterday, hours before her demise."

The blood drained from Millie's face as she recalled the unpleasant exchange. "It's true. Delilah showed up outside my cabin. She said she was interested in purchasing my home. She said several unpleasant things and I escorted her to the exit."

"Now what?" Millie had a sinking feeling she was in serious trouble. "Are you here to arrest me?"

"No." Patterson shook his head. "You haven't been charged with anything. We're in the middle of the ocean. We won't reach our first port stop, San Juan, until tomorrow. We've already arranged for Mr. Sanders and family members to disembark there. The body will be transported to Michigan where an autopsy will be performed."

Patterson waved her down the hall. "Let's talk in my office. I'd like to go over what you remember about your argument with Ms. Osborne and specifically, if you have an alibi for your whereabouts late last night."

They walked silently down the long corridor. Millie's steps dragged and she felt as if she were going to her own execution. Perhaps Roger had gotten into an argument with Delilah, plotted to taint her food and then, in a final act of revenge, decided to frame his ex-wife. He could kill two birds with one stone...end his relationship with Delilah and set his ex-wife up to take the fall.

Patterson unlocked his office door and held it open as he waited for Millie to step inside. "Have a seat."

Millie slid into the seat closest to the door and placed her head in her hands. "I can't believe this. I had no idea the woman had allergies."

Patterson eased into the chair behind the desk and opened the side desk drawer. "Unfortunately, Millie, it would be easy for you to find out with your clearance level. The fact that one of your closest friends, Annette, is Director of Food and Beverage also gives you access to the information."

Millie's head shot up. "You can't possibly think Annette is in any way involved."

"I don't." Patterson sighed heavily. "I don't think you had anything to do with the woman's death, nor do I think any other staff or crew had anything to do with it, but unfortunately, some of the evidence is pointing right at you."

"Motive and opportunity," Millie said.

"Tell me everything you can remember about your encounter with Ms. Osborne, from the moment she stepped on board the ship."

Millie recounted every detail she could think of until the moment she slammed the door behind Delilah after she exited the I-95 crew area. The more she talked, the more she realized everything did point to her. She was a bitter ex with an ax to grind. The only problem was, Millie didn't kill the woman.

Patterson finished jotting down his notes and placed his pen on top of the notepad. "We'll do whatever we can to clear your name, Millie, before the family disembarks."

"And the murderer walks off this ship, scot free," Millie said. "What if it was an accident? What if it wasn't intentional?"

"We're looking at every angle. We've started a thorough investigation which includes questioning family members and other witnesses," Patterson said. "You need to steer clear of this investigation, Millie. You're too close this time."

"You got that right," Millie muttered as she pushed the chair back and stood. "I still have a right to talk to my daughter and family."

"Of course," Patterson stood. "I'm probably wasting my breath, but could you please give us time to do our job?"

"I'll try," Millie said. "That's all I can say." She stepped into the hall and quietly closed the door behind her.

***

"Whew!" Annette blew air through thinned lips. "I heard. Patterson was here earlier and wanted to know who was delivering deck ten room service last night."

Annette drummed her fingers on the kitchen countertop. "Carmen was in charge of room service from nine p.m. til two a.m. for that deck of the ship. I'm sure Patterson has already talked to her."

"With all of the room service orders, do you think she'll remember who placed the order?" Millie asked.

"The crew is required to keep a written log." Annette shifted to the side and then turned back. "We usually keep it over here on the wall. I'll need to wait until Amit shows up for his shift to ask him where he put it. Patterson didn't ask for it but I'm sure it'll be next."

"In the meantime, I'll see if I can get my daughter, Beth, alone and ask her what in the world she thinks happened." Millie glanced at her watch. "I missed my early risers Sunrise Stride so I better get a move on."

"Don't worry, Millie," Annette said. "I'll help in whatever way I can."

Millie attempted a small smile. "Thanks. It looks like I'll need all the help I can get. I better go change into my work uniform."

After swapping out her workout clothes for her work uniform, Millie made her way to Andy's office. She could tell from the look on his face he'd already heard. "I know I told you it was boring and quiet while you were gone but you didn't have to kill your ex-husband's bride-to-be just to liven things up."

Millie sucked in a breath and slid into the chair next to Andy. "I can't believe she's dead. I had nothing to do with it. True, I didn't care for her, which may be an understatement, but I did not kill her."

"Did you know she was allergic to nuts?"

"Nope. Not a clue, although Patterson pointed out it would be easy for me to get that kind of information," Millie said. "Motive and opportunity. I'm the perfect person to frame."

"Patterson and his men are working on it Millie." Andy shuffled the papers on his desk. "In the meantime, try not to dwell on it. Spend your free time with your family and let the experts handle the rest."

"In other words, steer clear of the investigation," Millie said.

"You took the words right out of my mouth," Andy said. "Now if only you'll heed my advice." He changed the subject and they discussed the upcoming mystery/scavenger hunt, which had been rescheduled for the following day.

"You don't have to reschedule it." Millie was looking forward to the scavenger hunt and taking her mind off her current situation.

"We have enough activities today and I've already sent out the revised schedule."

They discussed the rest of the schedule and after they finished going over everything, Millie stood. "I better head upstairs if I'm going to make it in time to host trivia." She turned to go.

"Millie," Andy said.

Millie swung back around.

"Stay out of trouble."

"I'll try," Millie sighed. "Sometimes it seems as if trouble follows me wherever I go."

***

The trivia contest was a foodie's dream and Millie learned something new. She had no idea there were sixteen different ways to cook an egg. The most interesting was the tea egg, a traditional Chinese snack, made by cracking hard-boiled eggs and steeping them in a spiced tea mix.

A group of quilters, who had sailed together, easily won the trivia contest. Andy had switched out the contest winners' gifts, a ship on a stick, for a medallion necklace with the ship's name etched in the center.

The crowd dispersed as Millie placed the trivia items in the cabinet and locked the door. The talk of food made her hungry and she realized she'd missed breakfast so she headed to the crew dining room to avoid running into Roger.

Lunch consisted of rubbery hot dogs, hamburgers that reminded Millie of hockey pucks and a concoction she guessed was a Sloppy Joe mix.

She grabbed a hot dog and bun and then layered the top with mustard, mayo, sweet relish and a scoop of the Sloppy Joe mix for good measure.

She dumped a handful of tortilla chips off to the side, along with a small pile of semi-crisp French fries and headed toward the dining area.

Nikki, one of Millie's friends who worked at guest services, caught her eye and waved her over to her table. Sarah, Millie's old cabin mate, sat next to Nikki.

Nikki watched as Millie emptied her tray and set the empty tray off to the side. "You sure know how to spice things up around here."

Millie rolled her eyes and reached for a fry. "You heard."

"All of the crew on board has heard. Apparently, Mr. Sanders, your ex, was down at guest services causing a ruckus, demanding they arrest you."

The tips of Millie's ears burned. "You're kidding."

"Nope." Nikki shook her head. "I wasn't there but Anna, one of the other workers, told me about it."

"What happened?" Millie placed the half-eaten fry on her plate. Her appetite had vanished.

"I heard security arrived as soon as he started yelling and they led him away."

Sarah reached over and patted Millie's arm. "Don't worry. I'm sure they'll clear your name soon."

"I hope so." Millie stared at the food on her plate.

"You better eat, Millie," Sarah urged. "You can't let this get you down. We all know you had nothing to do with the woman's death. From what I heard, she was a real trip."

"She was." Nikki lifted her drink glass and sipped. "She came down to guest services yesterday at least twice that I know of, complaining about the pillows, the air conditioning. She even complained about the television channels."

"I'm so distracted I almost forgot to pray." Millie lowered her head and whispered a small prayer of thanks before she picked up her hot dog and bit the end. She forced herself to eat the food and listened as Nikki and Sarah attempted to distract her with tales of ridiculous passenger complaints.

Millie finished her food but the hot dog sat in the pit of her stomach, threatening to come back up. All she could think was someone was going to get away with murder and she was on the hook for Delilah's death.

Chapter 5

Millie peeked around the corner of the hall wall in the direction of her daughter and family's cabin. The coast was clear and the hall empty so Millie hurried to their cabin.

She tapped lightly on the door but no one answered. Millie fumbled inside her jacket pocket, pulled one of the pads of paper and pens she'd used for the trivia game from her pocket and jotted a quick note to Beth, asking her to contact guest services and have her paged when she returned to her room.

Millie folded the small piece of paper in half and shoved it under the door.

"You!" Millie froze at the sound of her ex-husband's voice. "You should be in jail. What are you doing here?" he growled.

Millie straightened her back and slowly turned to face the man she had once loved but now loathed. "I am looking for my daughter and, in case you forgot, I work on this ship. What I'd really like to know is what are *you* doing here?"

All of the unhappy moments her ex-husband had put her through came flooding back. She was about to unload on him when she caught a glimpse of Beth, hurrying down the hall.

Beth stepped between her parents in an attempt to diffuse a tense situation. "This is not the time or the place." Beth tugged on her mother's arm and led her down the hall, out a side door and onto the open deck.

Millie sucked in a deep breath, forcing herself to calm down.

"Dad is upset right now. He's convinced someone intentionally gave Delilah a peanut product. Delilah had told him about your confrontation earlier and now he's convinced someone helped you taint her food."

"Does he really believe I'm a killer?" Millie asked. "I was married to your father for many years and now all of the sudden he thinks I'm capable of murder."

"Well, not exactly." Beth clasped her hands. "He thinks you tried to get back at her but it went too far and ended up killing her."

"How exactly was I supposed to know she had allergies? Has he thought about that?" Millie began to pace back and forth.

"The chef cards were given to their room steward and also to the wait staff," Beth said. "He thinks you were in cahoots with them."

"And also the crew who delivered the room service," Millie added.

"Yeah." Beth sucked in a deep breath. "He's not thinking rationally right now."

"He hasn't for a long time," Millie muttered. "I know I didn't give her tainted food, which

70

leads me to believe someone close to her had it in for her."

"She is, I mean was, rather unpleasant," Beth admitted. "Not that I wished her dead or anything."

"I know." Millie squeezed Beth's arm. "I'm sorry you got dragged into this, sorry your dad had the dumb idea to board this ship and shove his nuptials in my face, but it's too late now."

"I agree," Beth said.

"If I didn't give Delilah tainted food and you didn't give Delilah tainted food, someone else did. We have to figure out whom and you might be able to help." Millie glanced at her watch. "I've got another 45 minutes before I have to head to the theater to host bingo. Let's go to the library where we can sit down and I can jot a few notes."

Mother and daughter headed back inside, and down to the Atlantic deck where the library was located. A group of guests sat near the window playing cards.

Beth and Millie headed to the opposite end of the room where they settled in at a table for two near the back.

Millie pulled the pad of paper and ink pen from her pocket. "Besides your father, Delilah, David, Noah and Bella, who else is on board?"

"Delilah's daughter, Linda, and her husband, Mike."

"Anyone else?" Millie asked as she jotted Mike's name on the paper.

"Her sister, Dixie, who acts just like her. Next is Dixie's husband, Elroy. He did not get along with Delilah at all." Beth plucked her cell phone from her pocket. "Before the...incident...I took get a picture of Dixie and her husband."

Millie studied the picture Beth had taken. In the picture was an unsmiling Roger, a beaming

Delilah, a woman who looked a lot like Delilah and another man. "I see the resemblance."

"There's another couple in the group," Beth said. "They're kind of odd."

Millie handed the phone back to her daughter and picked up her pen. "What do you mean by 'odd'?"

"They aren't very friendly and I get the impression they aren't happy to be on board the ship."

"Are they related to Delilah and Dixie?"

"I don't think so. That's the weird part. Delilah never formally introduced them or explained who they were," Beth said. "When I asked Dad who they were, he shrugged and said he thought they were old friends."

"Do you remember their names?" Millie asked.

"Ron and Julie Bosko, I think. He's some sort of pharmaceutical rep or something. Not sure what she does," Beth said.

Millie leaned back in her chair. "Our list of suspects. A sister who acts like Delilah. A brother-in-law who didn't like her, Delilah's daughter, son-in-law and two oddball friends."

"That about sums it up." Beth stood. "I better head back to the cabin. David took the kids to play miniature golf. I'm sure they're done by now and wondering what happened to me."

Millie trailed behind her daughter as they made their way to the door. "What does David think of all this?"

"He's as freaked out by the entire thing as I am. We both know you had nothing to do with Delilah's death." Beth reached for the door handle. "Is it possible the crew cross contaminated the plate of food and it truly was an accident?"

"It's possible," Millie said. "The late night kitchen crew might not have seen the chef cards or been told about Delilah's severe peanut allergies." Millie paused. "You would think someone who had that extreme of an allergy would be carrying one of those pens in case of accidental ingestion."

"That's what I thought, too." Beth shrugged. "Maybe she forgot it or it was too late by the time she realized she was having a severe reaction."

They stopped near the entrance to the theater where the bingo session was about to begin. "Are you going to get off the ship when we reach San Juan?"

Beth grimaced. "David and I haven't decided yet. On the one hand, we don't want to appear callous and uncaring. Dad is taking Delilah's death hard."

"Yeah and he's taking it out on me," Millie said.

"On the other hand, we weren't exactly close to Delilah and there's nothing we can do. What do you think we should do?" Beth asked.

Millie chose her words carefully. "I think you should be there for your father. If he wants you to be with him, then you should."

"I would rather stay," Beth said. "I want to do whatever I can to help clear your name. I can't do that if I'm on my way back to Michigan. My brain is fuzzy right now and I think I'm in shock. In the meantime, I'm going to try to pay closer attention to what the family and friends are saying and how they're reacting."

"Actions speak louder than words." Millie hugged her daughter. "Thank you, Beth, for believing I had nothing to do with Delilah's unfortunate demise. And thank David for sticking by me, too."

Millie waited until Beth disappeared inside the elevator and the doors closed before making her way into the theater. She patted her pocket and the list of family and friends who were on board the ship with Delilah.

She hadn't written Roger's name on the list, but perhaps she should have. Perhaps he'd purchased a large life insurance policy in Delilah's name.

She wondered why Elroy, Delilah's brother-in-law, disliked her. But then again, maybe she didn't wonder why.

There was also the odd couple, the friends, Ron and Julie something. How did they fit into the picture? Beth commented her father didn't know them that well, but Delilah obviously knew them well enough to invite them to cruise with them and attend their intimate wedding ceremony on board the ship.

Millie had a sneaky suspicion there was more to the "friends" than met the eye. She vowed that later that evening, after she finished working her shift, she would log onto one of the ship's computers and see if she could find anything out about the friends on social media.

She would have to move fast if she planned to do any poking around into the wedding party before they exited the ship.

Millie also needed to see if she could chat with Carmen, the crewmember who delivered the room service tray to Roger's suite, as well as look at the order itself.

She tugged on the bottom of her uniform jacket, straightened her shoulders and marched into the theater for the first round of bingo. There was no way Millie Sanders was going to take the fall for this murder, not if she could help it!

Chapter 6

"I tell you the truth, Miss Millie," Carmen said earnestly. "I knock on the door to suite 1027. The suite - it right near the service elevator. A blonde woman, she answer the door and take the food but she not very nice."

"You're sure it was suite 1027?" Millie asked.

"Yes. She very rude," Carmen said in broken English. "She give no tip and slam the door in my face."

"Sounds about right," Millie muttered. "Do you remember anything else, anything at all? Was there anyone else inside the cabin?"

"I remember she place big order and also order the sweet surprise. The guests, they pay extra for that." Carmen ticked off what it included. "It have red velvet cupcakes, frosted sugar cookie snowmen, chocolate chunk cheesecake, my favorite and also cream puffs."

"They so good." Carmen patted her stomach. "She take the tray so fast and shut the door, I see nothing inside."

Millie pulled Annette's clipboard toward her. Clipped to the front was the log sheet of late night room service orders for the previous evening. She slipped her reading glasses on. "It says here suite 1027 ordered a turkey wrap, minus mayo with extra lettuce and tomato." She squinted her eyes. "Absolutely no onions."

Millie shook her head. "Assorted vegetable sticks with blue cheese dressing, potato chips and the Christmas sweet surprise." She shifted her gaze. "Does this sound correct, Carmen?"

"Yes, Miss Millie." Carmen nodded. "I check the order before it leave the kitchen. I check all orders before delivering because sometimes they're wrong and I have to return to the kitchen to get the right order."

Annette, who had been listening in, piped up. "Did you, at any time, leave the food unattended between the time you left the kitchen and delivered it to the suite?"

"I had three other deliveries on deck ten," Carmen said. "I leave the food cart in the service area, just outside the crew elevators, deliver the first order, come back for the second and then deliver the final order."

"So it's possible the tray was left unattended for a short amount of time?" Millie asked.

Carmen nodded and her eyes grew wide. "There is no way to carry them all at once."

Millie patted Carmen's arm. "It's okay Carmen. We understand. We're just trying to figure out if someone may have tampered with the tray before it reached Ms. Osborne's suite."

Annette rubbed the bottom of her chin thoughtfully. "Nothing on the order was even close to having peanut product."

She turned to Carmen. "Did your paperwork note the passenger chef cards or allergies?"

"Yes." Carmen nodded. "It was in big letters across the front of the order. I make sure to keep the ticket with the order when I deliver so I don't mix up the delivery. I take the lid off each dish to check before delivering."

It sounded as if Carmen had done exactly what she was supposed to. She'd checked the order before it left the kitchen, double checked the order before delivering it to Roger and Delilah's suite and handed it off to Delilah.

Perhaps Roger had slipped the nut product into Delilah's food. Wouldn't that take the cake? Millie was certain Roger, a retired private investigator, was already conducting his own investigation.

Millie offered up a small prayer for Delilah, her family and even said one for Roger. A wave of guilt washed over her for all the awful thoughts she'd had since Roger and Delilah had boarded the ship.

She thought she was over the anger. For the most part, she was, but when it was right there in her face, taunting her, it was hard not to be bombarded with a slew of emotions, especially considering the fact that Roger and Delilah had intentionally boarded the ship to rub their wedding in Millie's face, at least that was her thought.

Millie eased off the stool. "I better get back to work. It's almost time for Pierre's wine tasting on deck six. Thanks for stopping by to talk to us, Carmen."

"I hope they clear your name Miss Millie. I don't understand how they think you had anything to do with the woman's death."

"Me either Carmen." She nodded to Annette and strode out of the galley. Today was a full day at sea and most of tomorrow would be, too, until they docked in San Juan the following afternoon.

It was becoming clear to Millie she would need Beth's help if she was going to get to the bottom of Delilah's tainted food and who might have had it in for her.

Pierre and Millie quickly assembled the wine tasting tables and tasting cups, along with an antipasto tray, which had been added to the event at Millie's suggestion.

She eyed the tiered trays of colorful offerings, including marinated vegetables—artichoke hearts, roasted red peppers as well as salty olives, rustic artisan breads, natural deli meats, small bites of seafood delicacies and rich cheeses.

The bite size snacks had been a huge hit with the guests. Millie picked up the tongs next to the tray and rearranged the offerings.

"Good afternoon ladies and gentlemen. I am Pierre LeBlanc, Siren of the Seas' Sommelier. This is my lovely assistant, Millie Sanders. Today we're going to visit the magnificent California wine country." There was a polite round of applause before Pierre got on a roll.

The wine tasting was one of Millie's favorite events to host. Pierre was part sommelier and part comedian and the crowd, as well as Millie, loved him. He was a smooth talking salesman, and Andy had told her they sold more bottles of wine during Pierre's wine tasting event than they did during the first half of a weeklong cruise. She could see why. He was charming, engaging and entertaining.

After the event ended, Millie helped Pierre clear the area. She hosted another round of afternoon bingo before she ran down to the theater to help Tara and Alison, two of the ship's dancers, with beginners tango lessons.

Millie had helped host line dancing and ballroom dancing, but she was having difficulty getting the hang of tango lessons. Maybe it was because each time she swiveled her hips, she was certain some part of her body was going to give out.

Still, she had fun working with Tara and Alison and the rest of Millie's afternoon flew by. She was starving by the time the lesson ended and Millie started down the side steps when she spotted Beth. She hadn't noticed her daughter sitting in the auditorium, watching.

"Hello dear. I didn't know you were watching."

"I didn't know you had moves like that," Beth teased. "Ooh la la."

"Guess I still got a little spunk left." Millie smiled. "So what brings you to my neck of the woods? Were you able to find anything out about our list of suspects?"

"Possibly," Beth said. "Do you have time to chat?"

"You're in luck. It's my lunch hour. Let's head up to the lido deck. Have you tried the deli yet? Their sandwiches are delicious."

Beth told her mother she hadn't and when they reached the deli, she ordered a smoked turkey on baguette while Millie ordered a toasted tuna melt.

"I have the perfect quiet spot. Follow me." Millie led her daughter through the side sliders, next to the deli station and to a cluster of bistro tables overlooking the ocean. After Beth returned with glasses of ice water, the women folded their hands and prayed.

"Dear Heavenly Father. Thank you for this food. We pray a special prayer for Delilah Osborne and her family, Lord. Thank you also for these precious moments I get to share with my family and for all of your blessings, my health, my friends, my job and most of all, my salvation. Amen."

Millie started to lift her head.

"And we pray the investigators are able to determine what or who killed Delilah so that my mom's name is cleared," Beth added.

"Amen," they said in unison.

Millie reached for her sandwich. "Have you heard anything new?"

Beth rolled her eyes and reached for a potato chip. "Dad is fit to be tied. He's threatening to sue the cruise line."

"Sue them?" Millie hadn't considered that angle, but it made sense.

"There was a minor incident last night when Delilah, Dad, all of us had gone down to listen to some live music near the center bar. We were munching on some appetizers from the *Appeteasers Snack Bar* and Delilah almost ate something with a trace of peanuts in it."

"Really?" Millie bit into her sandwich. "What kind of appetizer?"

"Sushi."

Millie wrinkled her nose. "Yuck."

"I agree but apparently Delilah loves...er, loved sushi. She noticed a faint odor and nibbled the edge of one of the pieces. All of the sudden she developed a rash on her upper lip."

"Wow! I had no idea. So now he thinks the cruise line was reckless and plans to sue?"

"Yep." Beth nodded. "I hate to do this to you, but David and I decided we're going to get off in San Juan and fly home with Dad and the others."

"I understand, Beth. It's the right thing to do. Your father needs you with him, even if it's just for moral support," Millie said.

Beth picked a piece of sliced turkey from her sandwich and popped it into her mouth. "Linda, Delilah's daughter and Dixie, Delilah's sister, are both taking it hard. Their spouses don't seem to be fazed by her passing." She shrugged. "Maybe they're trying to stay strong for their wives."

"What about the other couple, the Boskos?"

"Now there's a couple of odd ducks," Beth said. "They plan to finish the rest of the cruise. They told Dad there's nothing they can do to help Delilah and they're unwilling to pay extra to change their airline tickets."

Millie picked up a potato chip. "What about your father?"

"I think he's bouncing back and forth between shock and rage. One minute he's going on about suing and the next, he's talking as if Delilah is still alive."

"Is he still blaming me?" Millie asked.

"Sometimes. It's a toss-up between you, incompetent crew delivering food, incompetent kitchen staff and careless cruise line. You name it. Everyone is at fault but him."

"I'm sorry you got caught in the middle of this," Millie apologized.

"For the record, I was against Dad and Delilah marrying aboard this ship in the first place.

Reading between the lines, it had been Delilah's idea. Today was to be their wedding day." Beth glanced at her half-eaten sandwich, pushed the plate aside and glanced at her watch. "I better go. I'm meeting David and the kids over by the water slides."

The women dropped their dirty dishes in the bin near the door and Millie hugged her daughter. "Thanks for the insider info."

"I'll keep my ears and eyes open, and will let you know if I hear anything else," Beth promised before heading down to the other side of the ship and the pool area.

Millie started up the steps to check on the VIP area when her radio began squawking. "Millie, do you copy?" It was Andy.

Millie plucked her radio from her belt, turned the volume up and pressed the side button. "I'm here Andy."

"We have a 911 emergency in the Sky Chapel and I need you to meet me there."

Chapter 7

Millie hustled to the Sky Chapel where Andy, Dave Patterson, Oscar, Patterson's right-hand man and Pastor Pete Evans were hovering inside the door, talking in low voices.

The conversation abruptly stopped as Millie approached. All eyes turned to her and her stomach churned. Judging from the looks on their faces, they were about to share something unpleasant.

"Millie." Andy looked at Patterson helplessly.

Pastor Evans put an arm around Millie and led her inside the sanctuary. Her first thought was that something had happened to one of her friends. Her second thought was something had happened to Captain Armati. "I-is what happened now?" she stuttered.

"Let's go to my office." Pastor Evan's small office was in the back, near the entrance to the chapel.

Millie followed him in. Andy, Patterson and Oscar trailed behind and Andy closed the door behind them.

"I called Mr. Patterson and Andy after I found this note tucked inside my office door." Pastor Evans handed a folded piece of paper to Millie.

Millie unfolded the paper and her eyes squinted as she attempted to read the sloppy handwriting.

"Dear Pastor Evans,

Thank you for meeting with me to finalize my upcoming wedding plans. Your attention to detail is greatly appreciated and I'm sure our ceremony will be an unforgettable event for both Roger and me."

"I would like to address a concern that is weighing heavy on my mind, which is my

husband's ex-wife, Mildred Sanders, Siren of the Seas' Assistant Cruise Director. The woman has been stalking me since I boarded the ship. She has also threatened me with bodily harm and I would ask you provide not only Roger and me with security before, during and after the event to ensure our safety, but also our guests."

The note was signed, *Delilah Osborne.*

Millie read the note twice in an attempt to let the words sink in. Her hand trembled as she dropped the sheet of paper on the desk. "I did not stalk Delilah," she insisted.

"Did you threaten her with bodily harm?" Patterson asked.

Millie wracked her brain as she tried to remember exactly what she'd said to Delilah the previous day when the woman had confronted her outside her cabin. "She showed up on my doorstep and we had words but I don't specifically recall threatening her." But Millie couldn't guarantee 100% she hadn't. She'd been so ticked off at Delilah, anything could've come out of her mouth.

Millie's mouth went dry as she stared at the paper. "Now what?"

"I showed the note to Roger Sanders. He said the handwriting is Delilah's and the note is legit," Patterson said.

"That puts another nail in my coffin." Millie placed her head in her hands and closed her eyes. "You might as well put the handcuffs on me now."

"The only reason we called you here was to give you a heads up but try not to panic. Mr. Sanders hasn't been cleared yet, either, nor have any of the other people on board the ship who knew Ms. Osborne," Patterson said.

Millie lifted her head and glanced at Pastor Evans. "I thought Captain Armati was supposed to marry Roger and Delilah, captain of the ship and all."

Pastor Evans slowly shook his head. "When Captain Armati found out who it was, he bowed out and asked me to officiate the ceremony instead."

Sudden tears burned the back of Millie's eyes. Somehow, she'd managed to drag the people she cared most about, right into the middle of her crisis. Her children, Captain Armati. She glanced around the room. Her friends. Millie's bottom lip started to tremble. "I'm so sorry everyone."

Andy put his arm around Millie's shoulder. The pent up emotions inside her let loose and she began sobbing uncontrollably as she wondered how things could possibly get worse.

Patterson leaned close. "I know you're devastated, Millie, but I also know you're a fighter. Don't let this get you down. We believe you. We know you didn't kill Delilah Osborne, but we still have to figure out who did, if, in fact, it wasn't an accident."

Millie lifted her head and swiped at her wet cheeks. "I love a good mystery, but I guess I don't love it as much when I'm the one under the gun."

"That's why we're here," Patterson said. "I'm still in the process of interviewing Delilah's family and the crew who had contact with the contaminated food."

Pastor Evans leaned across his desk and plucked some tissues from the tissue box before handing them to Millie. "The only reason we told you is we thought you needed to know."

"I'm sure Roger is gunning for my arrest, in fact he told me so," Millie said bitterly. "He was closest to Delilah. I would think he would be a prime suspect."

"He is," Patterson said. "Which is another reason I think he's gung-ho to pin her death on you. It clears his name."

"He does seem distraught," Oscar, who had so far remained silent, added.

"As well he should be." Millie twisted the tissue around her finger. "Now what?"

"Stay as far away from Roger and Delilah's family as possible," Patterson advised. "We don't need to give them any more ammunition to use against you."

"Thank you for letting me know what's going on," Millie said. "I'll do my best to steer clear of all of them, except my daughter and her family, of course."

Andy walked Millie to the office door. "Take another half an hour off or so to clear your head," he said kindly. He waited for Millie to exit the chapel before closing the door behind him.

Millie stared at the closed door, wishing she could be a fly on the wall and hear the conversation now. She wondered if they were just being nice but suspected her of tainting Delilah's food.

She could have...could have slipped into the kitchen and swiped a layer of peanut butter on

Delilah's food. After all, she was a familiar face in the galley since Annette and she were close friends.

She also could have snuck into Delilah and Roger's suite. Millie had a master keycard and was able to access every single passenger cabin on board the ship, but she hadn't. Whoever had done Delilah in knew what they were doing. They knew about Delilah's severe allergies, knew she'd ordered room service and even knew when it was being delivered. All of the clues pointed to Roger!

Perhaps a member of Delilah's family had noticed something odd between them. She'd already asked Beth to try to glean more information on the others. Millie hoped she could do it without casting suspicion on herself. The last thing she wanted was for Beth or her family to be dragged into the middle of the mess any more than they already were.

Millie forced the entire situation out of her mind and focused on work. The rest of the day passed uneventfully as she finished another round of trivia, co-hosted the hot dog eating contest on the lido deck and then headed backstage to help with last minute preparations for the evening's show, Heart and Homes.

The practice run was hilarious as several couples vied for one of the four open spots. Andy made the final decision and chose a newly-wed couple from New York, a couple who'd been married for little less than a decade from Iowa, a third couple, empty nesters from Millie's home state of Michigan and the final couple, Millie's favorite, an elderly couple who were on board, celebrating their golden anniversary. The couple lived in South Florida.

After the stage had been set and the passengers given the information on returning for the big event, Millie headed upstairs to the galley to see if Annette, whose army of informants were the eyes and ears of the ship, had heard anything.

Annette and her sidekick, Amit, were up to their elbows in flour and despite Millie's recent bad news, she burst out laughing when she stepped inside. Not only was the flour up to their elbows, it was on their faces and in their hair. "It looks like a canister of flour exploded."

Annette shot Amit a dark look. "Ahem. Amit here decided we could finish our pastry project even faster if we skipped the tried and true commercial grade mixers and used some high-powered turbo hand mixers instead."

Amit lowered his head but not before Millie caught a glimpse of a grin. "You should've seen it Miss Millie. It look like it snowing in here."

Millie swiped her hand across the counter and picked up a thin layer of flour. "Looks like you'll have some cleaning up to do."

Annette took a step back and brushed her hands on the front of her apron. "Now that you've got this under control, I'm going to chat with Millie for a moment."

She ushered her friend to the pantry, Annette's unofficial office, and they stepped inside. "I heard through the grapevine Pastor Evans found a note from your ex's bride-to-be asking for security for her wedding because you'd threatened her."

"Good news travels fast." Millie sighed. "I just heard myself. I was angry at Delilah but I don't recall threatening her to the point she felt it necessary to request security at her wedding ceremony."

"She sounds like a crackpot," Annette said.

"She was...not a nice person." Millie didn't want to speak ill of the dead, but the woman was not a nice person, but then, neither was Roger.

"I heard Patterson is leaning toward closing the case, calling it an accident, that Delilah had ingested the peanuts by accident of her own accord." Annette straightened a can of tomato paste on the shelf. "Did you know that if there's even a trace of peanut oil or residue on a dish, someone who has severe allergies and eats from the dish could experience a reaction?"

"I had no idea." Millie shook her head. "Perhaps it really was an accident. Unfortunately, I don't think my ex is going to let this go. He's talking about suing Majestic Cruise Lines."

"Where did you say you met this gem of an ex?" Annette waved a hand. "Never mind. We all make mistakes. At least you ended up with two wonderful children from the marriage. Speaking of that, what do they think?"

Millie told Annette that Beth and her family believed she had nothing to do with Delilah's demise. She even told her Beth was going to try to hang around Delilah's friends and family to see if anything popped up on her radar.

"Did you tell her what to look for?" Annette ticked off her mental list. "Shifty eyes, changing the subject, lack of empathy for the victim. All the suspect signs of criminal involvement."

"No." Millie frowned. "Shifty eyes, huh?"

"Also known as avoiding eye contact." Annette flipped the pantry light switch and they wandered out of the storage room and into the galley. "Lookin' good Amit."

The women passed by Amit and wandered to the galley door. "I'm experimenting with my *Homestyle Collection* and am trying a new recipe for chicken pot pie. Stop by later and you can taste test it for me."

"I'm sure it's going to be delicious," Millie said. "I finish my shift at ten. Is ten too late?"

Annette made a circle with her thumb and index finger. "Perfect. We'll see you later. Actually, make it 10:30ish. Tonight is our late night Mexican Fiesta Festival so I've gotta get some goodies up on deck and then clean up."

"I'll see you then." Millie finished her rounds and with time to spare before meeting Annette in the galley, she headed to the bank of computers located on the other side of the library. She settled into a station near the back and pulled out the slip of paper she'd jotted Delilah's friends and family names on.

After the computer warmed up, Millie typed in her password and clicked on the search bar. She came up empty-handed when she typed in Michael and Linda Foster, and got the same result with Dixie and Elroy Keebler.

Although Michael and Linda each had social profile pages, both had security settings and the only thing Millie could view was their names. The Keeblers weren't on social media.

She typed in Ronald and Julie Bosko and finally, something popped up. She scrolled through the search results and her eyes widened when she found an old Grand Rapids Press newspaper article. Ronald Bosko's name caught her eye. The article was dated July 2015.

"Local socialite Julie Tindler-Bosko and her husband Ronald Bosko, a local pharmacist and owner of South Street Drug Store located in downtown Grand Rapids, Michigan are currently under investigation for insurance and EBT card fraud."

Chapter 8

After reading the brief article, Millie typed Julie Bosko's name in several social media sites and discovered Delilah and Julie had been friends for many years, since college.

There was a collage of photos, mostly of the woman and her pets. There were a couple of her standing next to a man who looked familiar but then Millie saw a lot of new faces every single day and she decided he probably looked like any number of male passengers.

She wondered what kind of insurance fraud investigation the Boskos were involved in. Since the news story was over a year old, she also wondered if the case was still open or if the investigators had closed it.

After typing in several other searches, all dead ends, Millie gave up trying to find anything else on the investigation and logged off the computer.

Somewhere between the delivery of the food and the time Delilah ate it, someone tainted the food. If it wasn't the room service staff, who was it?

Millie thought about the layout of Roger's suite and wondered if there was a connecting door. Many cabins as well as several suites had connecting doors. The connecting doors were popular with large parties of families cruising together; they would unlock the doors so they could access each other's cabins without walking out into the hall.

When she reached the galley, Annette, Amit, Cat and Danielle were already there. "You're right on time. Were your ears ringing? We were talking about you." Annette leaned her elbows on the countertop.

Danielle pointed to a row of pastry dishes. "My timing is impeccable and now I get to sample the tasty dishes Annette and Amit have whipped up."

The group spread out around the counter and Annette slid a chicken potpie dish in front of each of them while Amit passed out napkins and spoons. Millie's mouth watered as she eased the tip of her spoon into the flaky top crust to let the heat escape. The smell of baked chicken wafted up.

She set the spoon on top of her napkin and folded her hands in front of her. "Someone else can take the lead on saying grace and if you could put in a good word for me, I would appreciate it."

The group bowed their heads and Cat began to pray. "Dear Heavenly Father. Thank you for this delicious food set before us. Thank you for bringing Millie back to us safe and sound. Thank you for all of my wonderful friends. We pray, Lord, you give Dave Patterson and the investigators wisdom and help in solving the mysterious death of Delilah and that Millie's name is cleared. Thank you most of all for Your Son, our Savior, Jesus Christ."

"Amen," they all said in unison.

"Dig in," Annette added.

Millie scooped a heaping spoonful of chicken, carrots, potatoes and peas from the center of the dish. She savored the creamy gravy and the crusty top as she chewed the goodies inside. "This is so good."

"I agree," Cat murmured. "You've got another winner, Annette."

"Winner, winner, chicken dinner," Danielle joked. "Seriously, I've never had pot pie before but this is delicious." She changed the subject. "So what's the plan?"

While they ate, Millie told them about her research on the computer and what she'd found on the Boskos.

"I think we need to take a closer look at them," Annette said.

"Not to mention Roger," Cat added.

Millie broke a piece of crust off the top of her pie, dipped it in the gravy and popped it in her mouth. "I think someone tainted the food after it was delivered. Somewhere between the time Carmen delivered the tray of food and the time Delilah ate the food."

"Remember Carmen said there were a couple times the room service trays sat unattended near the service elevator while she delivered to other rooms," Annette said. "She also told us she kept a copy of the special order with the dishes so she wouldn't mix them up with the others."

"So it's possible while she was delivering to another room, someone snuck into the delivery area and tampered with the food," Danielle said.

"I've never noticed the service elevators. Do any of you know where they are?" Millie asked.

"I do." Amit who had so far remained silent, piped up. "I deliver when we're slammed and Miss Annette make me go."

"You're a good man." Cat patted Amit's arm.

"Annette doesn't deserve you," Millie teased.

Annette frowned at Millie. "He does too deserve me. We deserve each other."

"I'd like to check out the area," Millie said. "As long as we don't draw attention to ourselves."

Amit shook his head. "This time of night, the only people who use it are maintenance staff and room service. I think it be okay. The service elevator is not far from the galley."

They finished their potpie dinners, rinsed the dishes and stuck them in the dishwasher.

Annette wiped her hands on the towel and hung it on the nearby hook. "Lead the way Amit."

The group exited the galley with Annette the last to leave as she shut off the lights and locked the door behind them.

The ship's corridors were quiet. Several late night venues were still in full swing as guests hung out at the late nightclubs, were up on the lido deck enjoying the Mexican buffet, watching the late night comedy show in one of the lounges or had retired for the evening.

Tomorrow was a mixed day with the first half at sea. The ship would arrive in San Juan later that afternoon. They were running out of time. If Patterson and his men or Millie and friends weren't able to figure out what had happened to Delilah Osborne, Millie would be on the hook!

Amit stopped abruptly in front of a metal door, only a short jaunt from the galley. The door was one Millie had never noticed before. On the front of the door was a small black keypad. He pressed several buttons on the keypad and after a loud beep, the door opened.

Behind the door was a narrow hall and at the end of the hall was a set of elevator doors. The doors were motion sensitive and when they got close, they opened automatically.

Amit stepped inside and waved them in. "It will be a tight fit."

Annette and Danielle squeezed in to the small space. Cat slid in after them.

Millie hung back as her claustrophobia kicked into high gear and her heart began to race. "No way! You know how I feel about elevators."

Annette grabbed Millie's hand and dragged her inside. "You'll be fine."

"That's debatable," Millie gasped as the door closed. The elevator jerked and a grinding noise filled the cramped space.

"It appears we may have maxed out the weight limit." Danielle pointed at a placard above the door. "The sign says maximum occupancy is three people."

After a couple more jerks, the elevator began making a dull grinding noise and shuddered to a stop but the doors didn't open.

Millie stared at the door, willing it to open. "Why isn't it opening?" She fought to keep from panicking as she wedged her fingers between the doors and attempted to force them open. "I think we're stuck."

Annette tilted her head and stared at the sign. "Yeah. We definitely have too many people in here." She shifted her gaze and studied the door. "You may be too close to the door, Millie. Let's try scooching back."

A chorus of groans went up as the five of them squeezed in even tighter. Millie inched back until she was leaning against Cat.

Amit, who was closest to the elevator buttons, pressed the open button. The elevator let out a low moan and the doors slowly opened.

"Thank you God!"   Millie bolted from the elevator. "Never again," she vowed. "I am never getting on another elevator again."

Annette followed her out. "We might've been stuck in there awhile." She turned her attention to the room. "This looks vaguely familiar. I think I was in here way back when I first started working on board the ship."

The tiny room was only slightly larger than the elevator. In one corner was a trio of bins. One container was labeled plastic, one labeled food and the third glass and aluminum.

There was a small stainless steel sink and a compact icemaker in the opposite corner. "The employees wheel the delivery carts into this room and then deliver the food to the passengers," Amit explained.

"This is also where they bring the dirty room service trays when they're done. There are two exits." Amit pointed to a door. "This door is used for this side of the corridor. The other door opens to the other side."

Annette opened the door and stuck her head out. "Suite ten thirty-two. Ten twenty-seven must be on the opposite side."

Cat opened the other door and stepped into the hall. "This side has the odd numbers." The group followed her into the empty hall.

"This way." Amit pointed to the left.

They passed by several cabins until they reached 1027. "This is it."

The group retraced their steps and re-entered the crew service area.

"It's possible while Carmen was on this side delivering food, someone else snuck in the other door."

"But how would they know, the 'poisonaire' if you will?" Cat asked.

"They would know if they ordered it," Millie said. "Roger might not have motive for poisoning Delilah, but he certainly had opportunity. I still wish we could find out if there's a connecting door in Roger's suite and if so, whose cabin it connects to."

"Nikki Tan might be able to tell us if there's a connecting door," Danielle said.

Millie glanced at her watch. "It's too late to find out tonight. I could head down there first thing tomorrow morning." Time was running out. The suspects and maybe even witnesses, including her children, would be departing the ship when they reached San Juan. "Beth would know too. I'm sure she's been inside Roger's suite."

Mother and daughter planned to meet up for an early breakfast while David watched the children. It would be their last chance to spend time together before Roger and the others disembarked for the flight home. "I'll talk to Nikki if Beth can't remember. We need to figure out if someone intentionally tainted Delilah's food before we reach San Juan."

Amit pressed the elevator button and the doors opened. "I'm heading to the crew quarters. Anyone else want a ride?"

Cat and Danielle nodded and stepped inside the small elevator.

"No way." Millie shook her head. "I'll pass."

"I'll keep Millie company," Annette said.

The two of them waited until the elevator doors closed before exiting the service area and making their way into the hall. "I wonder if Patterson took a look at the order log. I was gonna do that and completely forgot. Do you have a minute to make a run by the galley to take a peek?"

"Of course," Millie said. "Maybe if we can retrace Carmen's steps the other night, we can stumble on some sort of clue."

When they reached the galley, Annette fished her keys from her jacket pocket and unlocked the door. She flipped the light on and after they stepped inside, she locked the galley door behind them. "It's over here."

Annette pulled the clipboard from the wall and flipped through the loose sheets of paper. "That's odd."

"What's odd?" Millie stepped closer and peered over her shoulder.

"The order log from the other night is missing."

Chapter 9

"Missing?" Millie asked.

"Yeah. I was looking at it this morning and thinking to myself I would mention it to you to see if any of the other names on the list rang a bell," Annette said. "I didn't see the name Beth or David although I have no idea what their last name is."

"Volk. Beth's last name is Volk."

Annette shook her head. "I definitely don't remember seeing that name."

"What about Bosko or Keebler?" Millie asked.

"The old noggin isn't what it used to be." Annette tapped the side of her forehead. "I can't say for certain. There was a bunch of room service orders on the list. I'm better at remembering food than names."

"Patterson probably came and got it so he could go down the list of names looking for possible witnesses," Millie said. "The man is starting to cramp my style."

"That would be my guess." Annette hung the clipboard back on the wall. "There's nothing left to do tonight. If I were you, I'd talk to your daughter first thing in the morning. If she's got any of her parents' sleuthing genes, she could very well have picked up on something that might be useful."

Millie thanked Annette for all of her help, and waited in the corridor while her friend turned off the lights and locked the door a second time. "The next logical step would be to find out who may have had it in for Delilah."

"What if it was an accident, an honest to goodness someone in the kitchen contaminated the dish by accident?" Millie asked. "At this point, no one can prove I had anything to do with her death."

"True," Annette agreed. "From what we've heard your ex seems set on blaming you but from what you told me, the woman was not pleasant and she may have ruffled a few family or friends' feathers."

The women made their way to deck one and the crew quarters. "Maybe a good night's sleep will help clear our minds and we can think better," Annette said.

Millie agreed before she told her friend goodnight and headed to her cabin. Even if Patterson and the investigators decided Delilah's death was accidental, she wondered if, in the back of her ex's mind, her children's minds, there would always be a lingering doubt about her innocence.

Forty-eight hours ago she had no idea she would have to face her ex-husband again and have him rub his upcoming marriage to the woman he left her for in her face, but also plan to have Captain Armati, Millie's boyfriend, marry them. The irony was unbelievable. Now the woman was dead and Roger was accusing her of murder.

If it weren't so horrifying, it would be laughable.

"Millie, do you copy?" Millie's radio squawked. "She'd forgotten to turn it off after her shift ended, but she was glad she hadn't. It was Captain Armati.

"This is Millie. Go ahead N-Captain Armati." She almost slipped and called him Nic.

"I wondered if you had a moment to stop by the bridge before turning in for the night."

"Of course. I'll be right there." Millie did an about face and headed back up the steps. Judging by the tone in his voice and the fact it was late told Millie whatever he wanted to discuss was important.

Millie's fingers trembled as she slid her keycard in the slot and gently eased the bridge door open. She'd always loved visiting the bridge at night. All of the colorful lights from the computers blinked and it reminded her of Christmas lights.

Tonight she barely noticed as she hurried past Captain Vitale and made her way to the other side where Captain Armati stood staring out the window at the dark seas.

"Captain Armati."

The captain spun around at the sound of Millie's voice. "Thank you for coming on such short notice. I know it's late." He waved her toward the side bridge door. It led to a small walkway that ran the entire starboard side of the bridge. "We can chat out here."

Millie followed him out and waited for him to close the door behind them.

"I'm sorry to bother you, Millie," Captain Armati apologized. "I know you have your hands full with just coming back on board, not to mention your daughter and family."

"There's something else." Nic paused as if searching for the right words. "I spoke to your ex-husband earlier after he made a scene down at guest services."

The blood drained from Millie's face. "Good news travels fast."

Nic rubbed the stubble on his chin. "I had no choice. He demanded to speak with me. From what the staff said, he was blustering about a staff member who had killed his fiancée and insisted we were harboring a murderer."

"Did he name me specifically?" Millie asked, although she already suspected she knew the answer.

"Unfortunately, yes." Nic shifted his gaze and stared out into the darkness. "Donovan Sweeney heard the commotion, brought Mr. Sanders to his office in the back. That's when Donovan called me. Mr. Sanders has convinced himself you had something to do with Ms. Osborne's unfortunate demise. After Mr. Sanders calmed and finally left, Donovan and I both agreed we're worried about your safety."

"You think Roger intends to harm me?" Millie was shocked. In all the years she'd been married to Roger, he'd never shown signs of being abusive.

Beth hadn't mentioned a concern her father was so upset he might harm his ex-wife. Maybe he'd gone off the deep end after their split. Despite what everyone had told her, deep down, she was having a hard time accepting the fact Roger might actually believe Millie would intentionally harm Delilah.

They say you can live with someone for years and never really know them. What if Roger had taken out a hefty life insurance policy on Delilah, devised a plan to kill her during their cruise and somehow found a way to make it seem as if Millie, the jilted ex-wife, had plotted her revenge after discovering Delilah had potentially lethal allergies?

It would be the perfect crime.

"What do you want me to do?" Millie asked.

"I've already talked to Andy. We're taking you off active duty until we reach San Juan and your ex disembarks. You're free to move about the crew areas of the ship but I ask that you avoid all passenger areas of the ship."

Nic placed both hands on the rail. "I'm sorry," he said softly. "I know you don't like the idea but I love you and want to keep you safe. We all know you're innocent and plan to get to the bottom of this but in the meantime, we need your help."

Sudden tears burned the back of Millie's eyes. More than anything, she wanted to throw herself in his arms and bawl her eyes out, but Captain Vitale and other crew were in the bridge and had a clear view of them.

Instead, she stiffened her back. "I appreciate your concern." A sob caught in her throat. "I love you too and I'm so sorry." Certain she was about to burst into tears, she spun on her heel and hurried back inside.

She attempted a smile at Captain Vitale, who gave her a knowing look as she rushed out the bridge door. She didn't slow her pace until she reached the crew deck and her cabin.

Millie slipped her keycard in the slot and opened the door to her cabin. Danielle was already inside. "What took you so long? I've already been up on the lido deck and back."

"Annette and I stopped by the galley to take a look at the room service order log from the other night, which, by the way, is missing." Millie slumped onto the edge of her bunk. "Captain Armati called me up to the bridge to give me some bad news. Why? What's up?"

"When I got back here and you weren't here, I went up to the lido deck to grab a couple cookies from the Mexican buffet. As I was wandering around eating them, I noticed some people up there. I think they may be the ones who came on board with your ex and his peanut partner."

"Peanut partner?"

"Despicable Delilah, may she rest in peace," Danielle said.

"Danielle," Millie admonished.

"Okay. *Miz* Osborne. Anyway, if those were the folks who were with her, they sure have a weird way of mourning her death."

Millie shrugged. "There are thousands of people on board this ship. You could be wrong."

Danielle grabbed her cell phone off the desk, switched it on and tapped the screen. "That's why I snapped a couple pictures. I think this is the same woman I saw when I accompanied Roger and Delilah to their suite." She held the phone out. "Do these people look familiar?"

Millie slipped her reading glasses on and took the phone from Danielle. "Beth showed me a picture she'd taken of Delilah's sister and her husband."

The woman in one of the pictures looked like she was ready to burst into tears as she stood near the railing. Millie tapped the screen with the tip of her finger "This looks like Dixie, Delilah's sister."

She swiped the screen. The next picture was of a couple seated at a high top table, eating. Millie squinted her eyes as she studied the woman's face. It was the woman she'd seen on the social media site...Delilah's friend, Julie Bosko.

"The woman sitting at the high top table looks like Julie Bosko." There were only two pictures and Millie handed the phone to Danielle. "Did you happen to notice if Roger was up on deck?"

"Nope." Danielle turned the phone off and placed it on the desk. "I looked for him but as far as I could tell he wasn't up there."

Danielle stood. "I say we head up there. If they're still around, we can run a mini surveillance. Don't you think it's odd they were out and about?"

"Yeah, I do, but I promised to stay below deck until Roger and the others exit the ship in San Juan." Millie slid off the edge of her bunk. "I can't sleep right now even if I tried. Maybe if I stay out of sight, we can run up there for a quick minute, but after that, I'll have to stay below deck."

"Don't worry. I'll make sure no one spots you. I highly recommend the Mexican wedding cookies. They're delish." Danielle held the door and waited for Millie to step into the hall.

The Mexican Fiesta Festival was in full swing when Danielle and Millie arrived. The sound of loud Latin music filled the air and the makeshift dancefloor was filled with partying passengers.

A mirror ball hung over the dancefloor and beams of light bounced to the beat of the music.

The tune was familiar to Millie and one they played in the salsa dance class. She began to hum along as they made their way up the side steps.

Along one side of the deck were long buffet tables. The tables were filled with a taco bar and large bowls of tortilla chips, salsa, melted cheese and spicy ground beef. There was a tiered tray offering a tempting array of quesadilla wedges.

The dessert station was at the other end of the taco table. Millie assembled a taco and added some spicy salsa and sour cream to the top before sliding a Mexican wedding cookie and cinnamon cookie on the edge of her plate.

Danielle loaded her plate with food while Millie waited for her off to the side. She pointed at Danielle's plate. "You're going to eat all that?"

"Yeah. The potpie we sampled earlier is long gone." Danielle picked up a tortilla chip and dipped it in her nacho cheese sauce. "I saw them over there." She nodded her head to the left of the entertainment staff, who were dressed like a Mariachi band.

Millie eased past a group of partiers and stepped behind the band and Danielle followed behind. "I see them up on the next deck."

Millie lifted her gaze and spotted Julie Bosko. The man seated next to her had his back to them. "That's Julie Bosko and I'm guessing her husband." Sitting nearby was another couple, Dixie and Elroy Keebler. They both looked sad.

"I don't think we should get any closer," Millie said. "We can watch from here." The women took a step back and into the shadow where they still had an unobstructed view.

Elroy began rubbing Dixie's back and Millie nearly burst into tears as the woman swiped at the tears on her face.

Julie Bosko leaned close and whispered in Dixie's ear and Dixie nodded. "This is so sad," Millie whispered, close to tears herself.

Moments later, Beth and David appeared on the scene and Millie eased behind Danielle. "There's my daughter."

They watched as the group huddled close together, deep in conversation. It was a horrible situation for everyone...Delilah's family, her daughter, Roger.

"What's the 411 on them?" Danielle nodded her head toward the Boskos.

"That's the couple who owns the pharmacy and are...were under investigation for insurance fraud back in Michigan," Millie said. "According to Beth, they're kind of running under the radar. No one knows too much about them. Why?"

"Watch their body language. They seem indifferent, almost bored by the family's grief. It's not a normal reaction, especially if they were close to the deceased."

Millie shifted her gaze to Danielle. "What are you now, an expert in human behavior?"

Danielle shrugged. "I've dabbled in it in my past life. It helps to be able to gauge emotions before jumping into unknown situations."

She continued. "Your daughter is very empathetic toward the family. Your son-in-law."

"David," Millie interjected.

Danielle nodded. "He looks uncomfortable. As I said, the other couple appears to be somewhat indifferent." She tilted her head. "The man on the other side of the sister, you said you think he's the sister's husband? He looks stressed out."

"Why do you say that?"

"Because he can't decide if he should sit or stand. That and he's clenching his fists."

"I would be stressed out, too," Millie said. "His wife's sister just died and they're not sure if it was accidental."

"True." Danielle finished her last bite of cookie and eased her empty plate into the nearby dirty dish bin. "You gonna try to track down the room service log?"

"Yeah. I decided to ask Patterson about it in the morning." Millie cast one final glance at her daughter. "There's not much more we can do here tonight."

Millie let the young blonde lead the way as they stayed out of sight and headed down the side steps. "Have you analyzed me?"

"Of course. Most of the time you display a lot of nervous energy, like you always need to be doing something."

Millie contemplated Danielle's analysis. "You're right. I'm always trying to jump in and help others. For some reason, I have to fix everything and everybody."

Danielle snorted. "Which is why you end up involved in all the shipboard adventures."

"Same for you," Millie shot back. "Half the time I'm trying to save your hide or rescue you."

"True," Danielle admitted. "I'm more of an act now, think later type."

"Impulsive."

They reached the side stairs and bank of elevators. Danielle headed toward the elevators.

"I'll meet you at the bottom," Millie said.

"I'll beat you to the bottom," Danielle quipped. "Someday we're going to confront your fear of enclosed spaces and elevators." She patted Millie's arm. "Okay, I'll go with you."

"Maybe if elevators would stop breaking down on me, I wouldn't be so apt to avoid them."

They made it halfway down to deck two when Danielle spotted the ship's purser, Donovan Sweeney, coming up the steps toward them and she froze.

Chapter 10

"It's Donovan," Danielle hissed, her eyes darting around the empty hall.

The women didn't have time to make it inside an elevator, even if they'd wanted to. It was too late to try to go back up. Donovan's long legs would catch them in no time.

"This way." Danielle grabbed Millie's arm and pulled her toward a nearby restroom.

Millie glanced at the sign next to the door, *Men's Restroom*.

"But," Millie started to protest.

"We don't have a choice," Danielle said as she flung the door open. Beyond the first door was a second entrance door. They hurried through the second door.

Danielle put a finger to her lips and pointed at the nearest stall before dragging Millie inside and slamming the door shut behind them. She flipped the lock while Millie prayed no one would come in. She cupped her hands to Danielle's ear. "I hope no one..."

The sound of running water and whistling interrupted the rest of her sentence.

Millie's eyes grew 'round as saucers while Danielle clamped a hand over her mouth. Her shoulders shook as she tried to stifle her laughter.

The running water stopped and the sound of a hand dryer filled the room. After the dryer shut off, heavy steps echoed on the tile floor.

Millie didn't let out the breath she was holding until she heard the door click shut.

"That was a close call," Danielle whispered. She unlocked the stall door and eased the door open before she peeked around the corner. "The coast is clear."

The women tiptoed out of the men's bathroom and into the hall. A man and woman came toward them from the opposite direction. The man cast a puzzled glance at the "men's" sign on the door and frowned.

"Random cleaning inspection," Danielle said.

"Huh." The couple kept walking but not before the man whispered something in the woman's ear and she turned around and gave them an odd stare.

"Let's get out of here before we run into anyone else." Millie headed down the steps with Danielle right behind her.

"You would think Donovan would've turned in for the night," Danielle said. "Do the ship's officers stay up all night?"

"They could probably ask the same of us," Millie said breathlessly as they reached the last passenger deck and hurried to the "crew only" door. "I promised to stay below deck until Roger leaves the ship in San Juan and I intend to keep my promise, for once."

Danielle shrugged. "Don't worry. I'll take over the investigation."

"Now I am worried," Millie joked.

Danielle pretended not to hear her. "We need to find out if your ex's cabin connects to the others. We also need to find out a little more about the Boskos. They don't seem at all distressed over Delilah's death."

"We also need to find out whom else on deck ten ordered room service the other night," Millie said. "I can try to track down Patterson since his office is below deck and I won't be breaking my promise."

The women stopped in front of their cabin door. Danielle waited for Millie to insert her keycard and open the door. "How's about you lend me your keycard?"

Danielle didn't have the same level of clearance as Millie, which meant her keycard was not able to open passenger cabin doors, the door to the bridge, as well as other restricted areas of the ship.

"No way." Visions of Danielle sneaking into restricted areas using Millie's identification and keycard filled her head.

"Why not?" Danielle closed the door behind them and began to pace the floor. "I could sneak into Roger's room, you know, just for a quick glance. I could be in and out quicker than you can shake a leg."

"No. No. No," Millie said. As much as she appreciated Danielle's willingness to help, Danielle acted first and thought second. She glanced at her watch. It was after midnight and she was whupped. Tomorrow was going to be a stressful day. Millie still planned to meet her daughter, but instead of meeting in a passenger area, they would have to meet in the crew area.

Beth would get a firsthand look at how her mother and the other crew lived, an area of the ship most passengers never saw.

After making a mental note to call down to guest services in the morning to let the guest services employees know that Beth would be contacting them, Millie got ready for bed.

Despite her exhaustion, her mind refused to shut down and she tossed and turned for a long time before finally falling into a fitful sleep.

The next morning, she jolted awake and glanced at her small bedside clock. It was six a.m.

Millie slipped out of bed to use the bathroom. She splashed some water on her face, brushed her teeth and turned off the light before quietly exiting the bathroom.

She stood still as she listened for Danielle's soft snores but it was quiet...too quiet. "Danielle?" she whispered. Danielle didn't answer so Millie said her name again, this time a little louder. "Danielle?"

Millie shuffled to her bed, turned her small bedside light on and then took a step back as she peered into the upper bunk. Danielle's bed was empty.

"I must've been sleeping better than I thought," Millie muttered as she flipped the main light on. She reached inside the side drawer to grab clean underwear when she noticed her keycard and lanyard were gone.

Danielle's hot pink lanyard was sitting in its place. "Danielle!" Millie gasped. She plucked her radio from the charging station, turned it on and pressed the button. "Danielle Kneldon, do you copy?"

Silence.

"Danielle. It's Millie, do you copy?"

Still no answer. Frustrated, Millie slammed the radio down on the charger and picked up the phone to call guest services. Kim, one of the guest services staff, answered. She asked Kim to spread the word her daughter would be stopping by guest services, looking for her mother and to give Millie a call in her cabin when she showed up.

She also asked them to keep an eye out for Danielle Kneldon and to tell Danielle to call her ASAP.

Next, Millie dialed Andy's office but it went right to voice mail.

Millie also tried to reach Andy on his radio, and then glanced at her watch, sitting on the counter. Andy was in the middle of his early morning television program.

She grabbed her work uniform from the closet and stomped into the bathroom. "When I get my hands on you, Danielle, I'm going to wring your neck!"

After she finished getting ready, she headed to the crew mess hall for an early breakfast. Most of the first shifters were long gone and the place was nearly empty.

Millie placed a spoonful of watery eggs, a few slices of limp bacon, some dry toast and a spoonful of what she hoped were hash browns on her plate before pouring a cup of coffee.

She made her way to the nearest empty table and after settling in, she bowed her head and prayed God would help her today, that Patterson and his crew would uncover the truth as to what had happened to Delilah and, last but not least, that Danielle would not get in any trouble using Millie's keycard.

She lifted her head and watched as Cat wandered into the dining room. Millie gave a small wave when she caught Cat's attention and then waited until her friend arrived with her breakfast before digging into her own. "I'm surprised to see you down here this early."

Millie groaned and rolled her eyes as Cat settled into an empty seat across from her. "I've been banned from the passenger areas until we depart San Juan today because Roger is on a rampage." She explained that Captain Armati had called her to the bridge and asked her to remain in the crew area to avoid a run in with her ex.

Cat picked up her piece of bacon and bit the end. "I realize the man is probably consumed by grief but he shouldn't take it out on you. Not only that, who in their right mind would bring his fiancée on board a cruise ship his ex-wife works on and decide to flaunt it in her face by getting married?"

"I know." Millie sipped her coffee and studied her friend over the rim. She thought of Cat's abusive ex-husband, who was serving time in prison for her attempted murder. "Sometimes we don't make the wisest choices in choosing a mate."

Cat reached over and patted Millie's hand. "You shouldn't blame yourself for someone else's actions. Besides, people change. I think you're a great judge of character." She smiled. "After all, you picked me for a friend."

"Yeah, you're right." Cat and Millie's friendship had started out a little rocky but they had gotten through the rough patch and there wasn't anything she wouldn't do for Cat and she knew Cat felt the same.

"Since you're banished to the crew area, what can I do to help? I don't have to open the gift shop for another hour," Cat said.

"If you could track Danielle and my keycard down, that would be wonderful." Millie flashed Danielle's keycard, hanging around her neck.

Cat's eyes widened. "Danielle took your keycard?"

"Yep. She snuck out with it early this morning and left me hers." Millie grimaced. "I can only imagine what she's doing right now."

If only Millie knew!

Chapter 11

Danielle eased the cabin door closed and breathed a sigh of relief as it clicked shut. She wrapped the lanyard around Millie's keycard and shoved it into her jacket pocket. "This is for your own good," Danielle whispered at the closed door before she spun on her heel and strolled down the crew corridor.

She made it halfway to the exit when she ran into Brody coming from the other direction. He was in a hurry and almost passed Danielle before stopping abruptly in the middle of the hall. "Is Millie down here?"

"Millie?" Danielle asked. "Uhm. Yeah. She's in her room, feeling under the weather. Why? What's up?"

Brody stepped off to the side to let other crewmembers pass by. "I heard her ex has it in for her, something about his girlfriend dying and the ex is blaming Millie."

Danielle nodded. "Yeah. She's taking it hard."

"Well, I was gonna tell her, I remember the dead lady, Delores something."

"Delilah," Danielle corrected.

"Delilah." Brody repeated the name. "I'm not good with names." He pointed at his eyes. "Now a face? I'll never forget. Dave Patterson interviewed all the security staff and showed us a picture of the woman. At first, I didn't recognize her. I guess it was because the woman wasn't wearing a ton of makeup, that's why, but then I got to thinking about it and I do recognize her."

Danielle leaned in. "How?"

"Well, my shift the other night covered the casino," Brody explained. "Sometimes I work the nightclubs, but one of the other security never showed up so they called me to work there. The place was hopping. The first night is usually the busiest. So I'm makin' my rounds and some big mouth woman starts screamin' she won. A crowd gathered around her and the casino staff came over to check."

"When the casino technician checked the machine, he said it had malfunctioned and they tried to explain to her she hadn't won. The lady went berserk, screaming she was going to have the technician fired. The worker said a few words to the woman he shouldn't have and the casino host escorted him from the area."

Brody continued. "A man who had been playing the machine behind her, started to argue with the casino host after he returned and raised such a stink I had to escort both of them out of the casino."

"And you think the woman was Delilah Osborne?" Danielle asked.

"I'm almost certain." Brody nodded. "I stopped by Patterson's office to tell him but he's not there so I figured since I was down here, I would let Millie know, too."

"Do you remember who the technician was who argued with the woman?"

"I can see his face but like I said, I'm not good at names," Brody said.

Danielle fiddled with Millie's lanyard, tucked deep inside her pocket. "There are cameras in the casino." Danielle was thinking aloud.

"Yeah. Everywhere. I'm sure they caught everything on camera." Brody scratched his chin thoughtfully. "I bet they still have a copy of the malfunction ticket locked up in the casino."

"Not to mention a shot of the worker who argued with the woman," Danielle mused. She glanced at her watch. "It's six-fifteen." She lifted her gaze. "What time does the casino open?"

Brody scrunched his brows. "Casino slots open at nine. The tables open at noon. Why?"

"I'm thinking we should take a run through there, you know, check it out." Danielle started toward the exit.

Brody trailed behind. "There's not much to see on the floor and we don't have clearance to go behind the counter."

You do if you happen to have a high-level clearance card like Millie. Danielle smiled brightly. "Tell you what, you show me which machine the woman was playing and leave the investigating to me."

Brody held the door and waited for Danielle to step through. He continued to protest as they headed to the bank of elevators. "There's nothing to see. The machines have been turned off and it's dark inside."

"Even better." Danielle stopped in front of a bank of elevators, punched the "up" button and waited for the doors to open. "All you gotta do is point out the machine the woman was playing when it malfunctioned."

They stepped inside and Danielle pressed the button for the seventh floor. When they reached deck seven, Danielle stepped into the hall. Brody stood inside, as if weighing his options.

"Well? Are you coming?"

"Against my better judgment." Brody lumbered out of the elevator and they made their way around the corner and into the corridor. "I'm on a tight schedule. I'm supposed to be at a safety briefing in twenty minutes."

"We'll work fast," Danielle promised as she picked up the pace.

They passed by the coffee bar, packed with early morning passengers. The tantalizing aroma of freshly brewed coffee wafted out. "I love the gourmet coffees but they're a little too pricey for my budget."

"I'm a beer drinker myself," Brody said as they passed by.

"At six thirty in the morning?" Danielle wrinkled her nose.

"No. Of course not. I usually drink prune juice with my breakfast."

"Good for you Brody. I'm sure it keeps you regular."

They passed by the casino bar as they entered the dark casino. Thankfully, the casino bar was closed and they slipped inside unnoticed.

There was a second entrance on the other side of the casino. Danielle walked to the other side and peered out. The corridor was empty. She headed back inside the casino where Brody stood waiting. "Where's the machine?"

"Over here." Brody wove his way past a bank of machines and stopped in front of an end machine, not far from the cashier counters. "This is it." He stuck his hand on the back of the chair. "It's a sevens machine. You have to get three or more in sequence. She got seven in a sequence and the lights started flashing but when the casino staff checked, the machine had malfunctioned."

Brody let out a low whistle. "She freaked out, screaming at the casino staff. They offered her a complimentary dinner for two at the steakhouse but the offer ticked her off even more."

Danielle tilted her head as she gazed at the machine. "How much did she think she won?"

"Ten grand."

Danielle crossed her arms. "No wonder she was upset. Would you rather have ten grand or a free steak dinner?"

"True." Brody shrugged.

Danielle shifted her gaze to the cashier counters. There were three service areas. Affixed front and center was a sign, '*Player's Club.*' "Where's the door?"

"Oh no." Brody started to shake his head. "We can't go back there."

Danielle pulled Millie's keycard from her pocket, careful to keep the front covered so Brody wouldn't see the card wasn't hers. She strode to the other end of the long counter and spied the door leading to the back.

"You better not," Brody warned.

Danielle ignored Brody as she slipped the keycard in the door and waited for the beep. Nothing happened. She tried again. "This stinkin' card is useless." She retraced her steps. "I guess we'll have to move onto Plan B."

"Plan B?" Brody asked. "What Plan B?"

"You'll see." Danielle placed both hands on top of the counter and pulled herself up. She slid forward on her stomach until she was able to grab hold of the other side.

Brody grabbed her feet, dangling off the edge. "You can't do that."

Danielle kicked her feet free and scrambled the rest of the way over. She slid sideways until she reached the other side of the counter and then hopped down. "Piece of cake."

"You're crazy," Brody sputtered.

"I've been called worse." Danielle dusted her hands off as she studied the casino cage. "Now I wonder where the recording equipment is..." She pushed a stack of binders to one side. "It has to be around here somewhere."

"You're going to get..." Brody was about to say "caught" when the tip of Danielle's shoe bumped a small knob jutting out of the bottom of the cabinet. Bright red and green lights began to flash.

Danielle's scalp began to tingle. "Uh-oh. What did I do?"

"You tripped the alarm. You're on your own." Brody jogged out of the dark casino and into the corridor.

"Coward," Danielle muttered under her breath.

Within moments, the place was swarming with security.

"You're not allowed back there." One of the security crew, who looked vaguely familiar, took a menacing step forward.

Brody placed both hands on his hips. "I tried to tell her that but she wouldn't listen to me."

"I uh..." *Think fast.* "I thought I saw a spark behind the counter, could've been electrical. Before I called maintenance, I thought I would check it out myself."

The security guard frowned. "Really?"

"Yeah. Uh." Danielle smiled. "False alarm." She hopped on top of the counter, slid across the top and dropped down in front of the security guard. "You never can be too careful with electrical equipment."

The security guard started to open his mouth and closed it. "If we catch you back there again, we're going to notify Dave Patterson."

Danielle raised both hands. "I completely understand." She hurried out of the room, but not before nudging Brody on her way out. "Traitor."

Chapter 12

The hours seemed to drag on as Millie hovered just outside her cabin door and watched the ship's crew and staff as they darted up and down the hall. She was bored, she was angry or maybe she was hangry. The meager breakfast she'd eaten earlier left a lot to be desired, but unless she could talk someone into bringing her some decent food, she'd have to wait until Roger and the others left the ship and she was allowed to join the others above deck.

Finally, the cabin phone rang and Millie hurried inside to answer it. "Hello?" It was Beth.

"Hi Mom. Guest services gave me the phone number to your cabin. Is everything okay?"

"I'll talk to you when you get here. You'll have to meet me in the crew area." Millie briefly told her daughter how to reach the crew deck and

Beth arrived at the crew area's main entrance a short time later.

"Have you been fired?" Beth asked.

"No. Follow me." She led her daughter to her cabin and closed the door behind them before offering her daughter the only chair in the place.

Millie briefly explained how Beth's father had raised a stink down at guest services, insisting Millie was responsible for Delilah's death and he wanted her arrested. "So Nic...Captain Armati asked me to keep a low profile, as in below the water line profile until your father exits the ship."

She didn't mention to her daughter that she'd seen her up on the lido deck the evening before, comforting Dixie, Delilah's sister. "What do you think, I mean...how are the others taking Delilah's death, besides your father?"

"Other than Dad, Linda seems to be taking Delilah's death the hardest. Delilah's sister, Dixie, is taking it hard, too. She's also threatening to sue everyone. Sue the cruise line, sue the captain, sue the medical staff."

"That sounds about right, especially if she and Delilah were a lot alike." Millie remembered how Roger and Delilah had met. Delilah's first husband had made a small fortune in investments and hid it in overseas bank accounts. When Delilah found out, she took him to the cleaners and ran off with Roger.

Millie kept quiet on her thoughts, not wanting to drag Beth's father through the mud, the complete opposite of what he was doing to her. She wanted to leave the entire thing...and him...in the rearview mirror, or in this case, at the pier.

"What about the spouses?" Millie asked. "Delilah's brother-in-law, son-in-law, the Boskos?"

Beth wrinkled her nose. "If they're mourning, they're doing it internally. I have to say that it's odd none of them seem particularly distraught."

Beth scooted her chair closer to her mother and the bunk. "I'm sorry I didn't warn you ahead of time and I'm sorry we're not staying on."

Millie leaned forward and hugged her daughter. "Don't be sorry. You're doing what you think is best and I know you would've done the same for me."

"I better get back to the cabin to pack. The security people are going to get us and...Delilah...off the ship first." Beth stood. "It looks like we're going to spend the night in San Juan and fly out tomorrow morning. The cruise line booked us into a hotel right near the port. At least we got to spend time together while you were on break."

Millie walked her daughter out of the cabin and to the crew exit door. "Oh! I did think of one thing I meant to ask you. Do you know if anyone else's cabin has a connecting door with your father's suite?"

Beth stopped. "I'm not certain." She shook her head. "No. Now that I think about it, none of the cabins connected to Dad and Delilah's suite. We're all right in a row. David, me and the kids, Dad and Delilah, Dixie and Elroy and then Mike and Linda."

Beth snapped her fingers. "Oh, and the Boskos are right across the hall from Dad's suite."

Millie held the door and waited for Beth to step into the corridor. Tears burned the back of Millie's eyes as she wondered when she'd see her daughter again. It could be months.

Beth's lower lip began to quiver. "I'm sorry Mom."

Millie hugged her daughter. "We'll see each other again, before you know it." She mustered a small smile and when the door closed behind her daughter, Millie stifled a sob as she reminded herself this was her decision, her choice to work on board the cruise ship.

Determined to track down the room service log of orders, Millie blinked back the tears, squared her shoulders and marched down the hall to the other end of the ship and Dave Patterson's office.

Patterson wasn't inside, but Oscar was there. He was sitting in Patterson's chair, his feet propped up on the desk. When he caught sight of Millie, he quickly yanked his feet of the desk and sat upright. "Miss Millie."

"Hello Oscar." Millie slipped inside the office. "I was hoping to talk to Patterson but you might be able to help me."

"How?" Oscar, familiar with many of Millie's previous unauthorized investigations, eyed her with suspicion.

"I believe Mr. Patterson has the room service order log sheet from the night Ms. Osborne died. I was wondering if I could take a quick look at it."

Oscar's eye slid to the stack of dividers off to one side. "I'm not sure he still has it."

Millie eyed the dividers. "Mind if I take a look through his file organizers?" She didn't wait for a reply as she leaned over the desk and began shuffling through the stack of papers.

"You shouldn't be doing that." Oscar lunged forward to stop her.

"Ah. I see it here." Millie snatched the small stack of clipped papers from his reach and pulled them close to her face. She didn't have her reading glasses with her and she squinted her eyes as she attempted to read the paper.

She quickly located Delilah's order and then scanned the list of names. Her heart skipped a beat when she spotted an order for Julie Bosko, placed right around the same time. *Side salad with ranch dressing, cookie sampler and a BLT on wheat toast.*

"I think I've seen everything I need to see." Millie handed the papers to Oscar who quickly shoved them back inside the organizer. "Please tell Patterson..."

"Tell Patterson what?" Dave Patterson stepped inside his office.

Millie shifted in her chair. "Have you determined a cause of death for Delilah Osborne?"

"I filed the report and it's officially been listed as an allergic reaction and accidental ingestion." Patterson ran a hand through his hair. "We met with Mr. Sanders and he does not agree with our determination."

"I heard he plans to sue," Millie said.

"Him and everyone else in his party. They're all threatening to sue." Patterson reached in his pocket and pulled out Millie's keycard and lanyard. "Does this look familiar?"

"It sure does." Millie took the lanyard from Patterson and slipped it over her head. "Danielle borrowed it early this morning without my permission. How did you find it?" She held up her hands. "Let me guess. Danielle was trying to access a restricted area of the ship."

"Our security caught her trying to snoop behind the casino's cashier desk and while they were questioning her, one of the guards noticed her keycard and realized it wasn't hers so they took it."

"Thanks." Millie shook her head. "Danielle's heart is in the right place and she's only trying to help but she sure can be a handful."

"Like someone else I know." Patterson gave her a pointed stare. "We reprimanded her but my guess is it went in one ear and out the other."

"Sounds about right." Millie changed the subject. "I see the Boskos, who were in a cabin directly across the hall from Delilah's suite, ordered room service close to the same time as Delilah. Is it possible they had something to do with Delilah's accidental ingestion?"

"I tried to question them. They both seemed agitated and their answers were vague," Patterson said.

Millie glanced at her watch. "I guess it doesn't matter. In a few hours we'll reach San Juan and my life will return to normal, whatever that is."

As Millie slowly walked back to her cabin, something...some small clue lurked in the back of her head, but for the life of her, she couldn't pinpoint what it was. Perhaps Delilah's death had been accidental. It wouldn't be the first time someone had ingested a substance they were highly allergic to and then died.

Danielle was waiting outside their cabin when Millie arrived. "Well, well, well. I suppose you're looking for this." She fished Danielle's lanyard out of her pocket and placed it into her outstretched hand. "Patterson gave me back my keycard, the one you borrowed without my permission."

Danielle dropped her lanyard around her neck and hung her head. "I was only trying to help. I did find something out." She told Millie the story Brody had told her, how Delilah had been in the casino and believed she'd hit a "jackpot" only to find out she hadn't.

Millie interrupted. "Which is why you were snooping around behind the casino desk."

"Yeah. A word of warning. Don't ever go back there. They have a silent alarm and I accidentally tripped it."

Millie grinned. "I would've loved to have seen the look on your face."

"Not funny." Danielle punched Millie in the arm and smiled. "I bet I had that deer-in-the-headlights look." She shrugged. "Security questioned me, found your keycard and then took it from me so I knew I was busted."

She continued. "Did you talk to Beth?"

Millie told Danielle what Beth had said. "They're going to be one of the first to disembark the ship. The cruise line booked rooms for them in a hotel near the port. They're flying out tomorrow."

"That's cool." Danielle flipped her blonde locks off her shoulders. "I say once they're off the ship, we head upstairs and check out their suite to see if they left behind any clues."

Millie closed her eyes. "I'm not sure if I'm up for it. Let me think about it." Danielle headed to Andy's office while Millie rambled around the crew area. She straightened the crew lounge and bar area before logging onto an employee computer to check her email and bank account.

Finally, Andy radioed to let Millie know the coast was clear and he wanted her to stop by his office.

Millie wasted no time as she hurried from the crew area. She slipped into his office behind the stage and settled into the seat across from him.

Andy pointed at her keycard. "I see you got your keycard back."

Millie nodded. "Yeah. Although Danielle's heart is in the right place, she just doesn't think before she acts." She changed the subject. "I took a look at the room service log the night Delilah was poisoned and noticed that the Boskos, friends of Delilah's, ordered room service around the same time she did."

Andy leaned back in his chair and crossed his arms. "A lot of people order room service after a night out and all of the restaurants and buffet have closed."

"True. I also did a little snooping around on the computer and discovered the Boskos were under investigation for fraud."

"It doesn't mean they're killers," Andy pointed out. "What motive would they have for killing a friend?"

"I have no idea. I'm stumped on that part. I think there's more to the Boskos than meets the eye."

"It doesn't matter now. Your husband and family have exited the ship. Captain Armati sent a staff member to accompany them to make sure they're settled in the hotel."

Millie's shoulders sagged. Although she was sad her daughter and grandchildren were gone and they would miss out on the fun day she'd planned with them on the island of St. Croix, the ship's next port stop, she was relieved she could put the whole incident behind her and get back to work.

Before Beth had left, Millie promised to call her daughter when they reached the next port to make sure they'd made it home safely and find out what else her ex had said. The last thing Millie wanted was for Roger to spring an internal cruise line investigation on her. At least if she knew ahead of time what he planned, she could brace herself for it.

Andy handed Millie her work schedule for the remainder of the afternoon and evening. It included a San Juan history trivia contest. After that was a "name that tune" game up on lido followed by the new "Cruise Clue" mystery/scavenger game.

"This looks great." Millie folded the sheet in half and shoved it in her pocket. "I'll have enough time to grab a burger before I start the trivia contest."

She hurried across the empty theater, down the steps and out the door where she ran into Danielle coming from the other direction. "Where you headed?"

"I'm going to grab a burger and then host trivia."

"I've got water wars with the two teens who didn't get off the ship," Danielle groaned.

"Two? That's it?"

"Well, maybe that's an exaggeration but there is only a couple." The women parted ways with Millie heading to the upper deck while Danielle headed to Andy's office for what Millie guessed would be a stern lecture about borrowing Millie's keycard.

After loading her lunch plate with a hot-off-the-grill juicy cheeseburger with toasted bun and all the toppings, she added a side of nachos, leftover from the previous night's Mexican Fiesta Festival and headed to a quiet corner, which wasn't hard to find. The majority of the ship's passengers had gotten off to explore the island.

Millie had toured old San Juan before her leave. Annette and she had visited the historic district, the Castillo San Cristóbal, also known as Fort San Cristóbal and Chapel of Christ the Savior (Capilla de Cristo), which was her favorite excursion on the island. They stumbled upon a pigeon park next to the chapel, all of which was a short walk from the pier.

Her plan had been to use her free hours when the ship docked in St. Croix. They'd booked a boat ride and snorkeling excursion to Buck Island, famous for its snorkeling and pristine, sandy beaches.

Her throat clogged as she thought about the missed memories with her grandchildren and chided herself for being so selfish. Roger was mourning the loss of his loved one. At least she still had her family.

After she finished her food, she glanced at her watch. She still had another half an hour before she was scheduled to host trivia.

Millie wandered to the gift shop to chat with Cat and then remembered the shop was closed while the ship was in port so she kept walking until she reached the galley.

She bounced up on her tiptoes and peeked in the round porthole window. The galley was a beehive of activity as staff darted back and forth around the large kitchen.

Millie wandered aimlessly around the ship until she found herself standing in front of the door to the bridge where she let herself in using her keycard.

First Officer Craig McMasters stood in front of the computer screen. He looked up when Millie approached. A slow smile spread across his bearded face. "Hello Millie."

Millie returned the smile. She loved the new officer's accent and had fun teasing him about his red beard. There was an easy manner about him and Millie had quickly decided he was a good fit for Siren of the Seas. "Hello Officer, er. Craig." Millie had never been certain how to address a first officer but First Officer McMasters had put her at ease, insisting she call him by his first name.

"Captain Armati isn't here right now," Craig said in his lilting Scottish accent. "He's got a meetin' with security I do believe."

Millie suspected Captain Armati had told his first officer about their relationship and she hoped it wasn't the only reason he was so kind to her. She didn't think so. "I understand. I just thought I would pop in now that..." Her voice trailed off.

"Your tormentor has exited the ship."

Millie smiled at the way he put it. "Yes, my tormentor has disembarked. Unfortunately, he took my daughter and grandchildren with him." She turned to go and then thought of something that would lift her spirits. "I'm going to stop by to say hello to Scout before I report to work." She stepped into the hall and to the door leading to the captain's private quarters.

Millie punched in the access code and stepped inside, quietly closing the door behind her. Scout barreled across the floor and pounced on Millie's shoe. She picked up the pint size pup and held him close as he licked her chin, her nose, her neck and then tried to bite her dangling earring. She pulled it away from his mouth and laughed. "Stop that."

She carried Scout into the living room and they made their way over to the slider. "I only have a minute. Would you like to go out?" Scout wiggled in her arms as she unlocked the slider and slid the door open.

They stepped out onto the balcony and Millie gently set Scout down. He promptly darted to his puppy pad and took care of business while she stood at the railing. From her vantage point, Millie had a bird's-eye view of the historic fort.

Off in the distance, she caught a glimpse of the San Juan skyline and wondered where exactly her daughter and family were staying. Millie shook off the melancholy mood and picked Scout up.

She talked to him for a few minutes and then set him back inside, locking the slider behind her. It was time to get back to work. She exited the apartment and the bridge, giving Craig McMasters a small wave before she stepped out into the hall.

Millie squared her shoulders. It was time to put Delilah's death behind her and focus on her job.

Chapter 13

The hours flew by as Millie flitted from event to event. It felt good to be back in the swing of things without having to worry about running into Roger or anyone else in his party.

She offered up a small prayer for peace for not only Roger, but also Delilah's children and her family and friends.

Because the ship's departure was scheduled for midnight and passengers were free to board until 11:30 p.m., the entertainment schedule was light for the evening. There was no headliner show. Instead, a classic Christmas movie was playing on the enormous movie screen, which hung above the main pool.

Millie passed by the deck where the smell of buttery popcorn filled the air. The movie was in full swing and she stood off to one side to watch for a moment.

A green furry creature with spiked bangs tiptoed toward a Christmas tree. She'd seen the classic Christmas show many times but for the life of her, couldn't place the name. As she passed through, she picked up empty popcorn bags and hot chocolate cups and tossed them in the trash bin.

"Millie - do you copy?"

Millie plucked her radio from her belt and held it to her mouth. "I'm here Andy. Go ahead."

"Could you please meet me near the gangway?"

"I'm on my way." Millie clipped her radio to her belt and hurried down the side steps. A knot formed in the pit of her stomach and she had a sinking feeling whatever Andy wanted had something to do with Roger.

She was partially right, and as she approached the gangway, she noticed Andy talking to a familiar figure. It was Beth. "What are you doing here?" She gave her daughter a quick hug.

"Dad forgot his blood pressure medicine in the dresser next to the bed. Mr. Walker said I could go back to the cabin and get it but thought you might like to go with me."

Andy winked at his employee. "I hope you don't mind."

"Of course not." Millie shot Andy a grateful smile. "Thanks for thinking of me. We'll be back shortly."

The women exited the atrium and walked past the bank of elevators. Beth, well aware of her mother's aversion to elevators, automatically headed toward the stairs.

"How is everyone doing?" Millie avoided mentioning Roger by name.

"Okay, considering the circumstances. The hotel is very nice. They booked each family in a separate suite. Delilah's daughter, Linda, and her husband got into a huge argument while we were checking in and insisted on separate rooms."

"I'm sure Linda is devastated by her mother's death. Her husband should cut her a little slack," Millie said.

"I agree but have done my best to stay out of it. Dixie and Dad are still talking about suing. If I didn't know better, I'd almost be tempted to think her sister has a huge life insurance policy out on her, the way she's going on and on."

"What about the other couple, the Boskos?" Millie asked.

"They decided to stay on board and finish the cruise." Beth grabbed the handrail and started up the steps. "I think Dad is relieved. He didn't care for them for whatever reason."

"Now that you mention it, I think you did tell me they didn't want to pay extra to change their airline tickets," Millie said.

They climbed the stairs until they reached deck ten and headed down the hall toward the suite. "Here it is." Beth stopped in front of the door marked 1027.

"If the stewards already cleaned the suite and found any personal belongings, they would have turned them in to guest services." Millie slipped her keycard in the lock and then pushed the door open. She fumbled for the light switch.

Bright interior lights illuminated the room. "That's better." They headed down the small hall, past a cozy sitting area and into the bedroom. "The cabin stewards haven't been here yet." Millie pointed to the unmade bed.

"Good." Beth stepped over to the small dresser next to the bed, opened the drawer and reached inside. "Here they are." She pulled out a prescription bottle and slipped it into her purse while her mother surveyed the room.

"You were right. There isn't a connecting door." Millie wandered past the bed and made her way over to the sliding glass door. "I wonder..."

Millie opened the slider and stepped out onto the deck. Tucked off to one side was a lounge chair. Two patio chairs sat next to the lounge chair and there was a small round metal table between them.

She shifted her gaze to the frosted white divider, which separated the balcony from the one next to it.

Beth followed her mother out onto the balcony and watched as she wandered over to the balcony divider and gave it a gentle nudge. The divider slid open. "I forgot these dividers can be unlocked and opened."

Millie's heart began to pound. "I wonder if the other one is unlocked." She retraced her steps, hopped over the lounge chair and pushed on the divider on the opposite side. It, too, swung open.

"Oh my gosh!" Beth gasped. "I remember you asking me if there was an adjoining door but I never thought about the fact Dad and the others unlocked the sliders so they could wander back and forth to each other's cabins."

Millie nodded absentmindedly as she stepped onto the adjacent balcony. She pushed on the slider handle and the door slid open. There was barely enough light for Millie to see inside the cabin. She flipped the lights on and gazed around the room.

Beth followed her mother inside.

"Who was staying in this cabin?"

"Delilah's sister, Dixie, and her husband."

The bed was unmade which meant the cleaning crew hadn't yet touched the cabin. The temptation to search the cabin was too great and Millie hurried across the room.

She stepped into the bathroom and quickly searched the medicine cabinet and drawers before moving onto the closets. The desk drawers were next. She finished by searching the nightstands on each side of the bed. "There's nothing here."

"If we hurry, we can do a quick search of Linda's cabin before heading back down. I don't want to take too long or Andy will wonder what happened to us."

When they reached Linda's slider, the door was locked so they circled back through Roger's suite and out to the hall where Millie let them in the cabin using her keycard.

Beth shuffled closer. "Do you have access to all the passengers' cabins?"

Millie nodded as she opened the door. "Yes and it has gotten me into hot water more than once." The women slipped inside and Millie quietly closed the door behind them.

The layout of the room was the reverse of Roger's and much smaller since it was a standard cabin and not a suite. Millie quickly found the light switch and flipped it on before opening the closet door.

"I'll search the bathroom." Beth stepped into the bathroom and began opening the cabinets and drawers while Millie searched the closets and dresser drawers. Their speedy search was in vain and the cabin was free of any personal belongings.

"This was a dead end," Beth said as she surveyed the cabin.

"Not quite." Millie pointed to the sliders and deck. "The three cabins connect, which means someone could have slipped into Delilah and your father's suite and tainted the cream puff." She wondered what Dave Patterson thought of the connecting balconies. Surely, he'd questioned the parties on both sides.

The women retraced their steps and exited the cabin. Millie shut the light off and pulled the door closed. "I have to say I don't agree with Dad when he says he thinks you may have been involved, but I do think the crew should be more careful with passenger allergies. I mean, first Delilah almost eats the sushi with some sort of peanut paste smeared on the bottom and from what we were told, her cream puff had a dab of peanut butter inside."

"I'm sure the investigators are looking into it." Millie made a mental note to ask Annette where they stored the cream puffs as she and her daughter walked toward the stairs. "What times does your flight leave in the morning?"

"The cruise line is still working on getting clearance to take Delilah...back to Michigan. Last we heard was early afternoon. You'll be long gone by then."

Millie walked her daughter to the gangway and said goodbye a second time. Beth gave her mother a small wave when she reached the bottom before disappearing from sight.

The connecting sliders cast a new light on the mystery surrounding Delilah's demise. Both Dixie and Linda would know of Delilah's allergies but if one of them intended to taint her food, why wait until they were on a cruise ship, in the middle of the ocean? Unless the plan was to pin it on the bitter ex who had both motive and opportunity.

An added bonus would be suing the cruise line for negligence! Someone in one of those other cabins had slipped a toxic substance into Delilah's food. Millie could feel it in her bones. Now all she had to do was figure out whom.

She climbed the stairs to deck seven and marched down the long hall to the galley. Millie peeked through the porthole window where she spotted Annette off in the far corner, standing inside the pantry.

Millie hurried inside and over to the pantry. Her friend looked up from the clipboard she was holding. "You look like you've got ants in your pants."

"I may be onto something. I think someone close to Delilah knew about her severe allergies to peanuts and intentionally tainted her cream puff."

"Why?"

"My guess is the motive was greed or jealousy and the opportunity, the connecting sliders between Roger and Delilah's suite. Dixie and her husband were on one side and Linda and her husband on the other."

"What about the others, the friends?" Annette asked.

"The Boskos? That's another thing. Perhaps Delilah had some dirt on them and was bribing them. By the way, they didn't get off the ship. They decided to stay on and finish their cruise."

Annette snorted. "With friends like that, who needs enemies?"

"Right?" Millie began to pace. "Maybe it was the Boskos. They ordered room service close to the same time. Follow me here. What if they were all hanging out on the deck and Delilah mentioned being tired but wanting to order room service before heading to bed? The Boskos or perhaps one of the others knew she'd ordered the food and waited for it to arrive. Somehow they managed to get their hands on the tray of sweets and tainted the cream puffs before Delilah sampled them."

Annette tapped her pen on top of her clipboard. "Carmen already told us she'd stuck the ticket on top, noting the order belonged to suite 1027. They could have slipped into the hall while Carmen was delivering another order."

"Or found an opportunity to taint it while no one was around," Millie said. "Roger left the cabin to get drinks and when he returned she was lying on the floor, clutching the tainted cream puff."

"I need to take a walk to clear my head." Millie shuffled backward and out of the pantry.

"I'll go with you," Annette offered. "Amit can cover for a few minutes." She hung her clipboard on the wall and followed Millie into the galley.

"Maybe we can stop by guest services to see if Nikki is around. She may have heard or seen something."

"Good idea." Annette turned to Amit. "Millie and I will be back in a few."

Amit smiled and nodded as the women zig zagged past the stainless steel counters and headed to the side door.

Annette swung the door open and it swung back, nearly smacking her in the face. She quickly stepped to the side and they watched as Nikki burst into the galley. "I've been looking all over for you," a breathless Nikki said as she gazed at Millie.

Millie fumbled with her radio, attached to her belt. "Did you try calling me on my radio?"

"Oh!" Nikki frowned. "Why didn't I think of that?"

Several of the kitchen staff turned to see what all the commotion was about and Nikki motioned them into the outer corridor. "I just left Dave Patterson's office. I got an odd call from a guest a short time ago. I kept thinking the name sounded familiar. It was one of the passengers Patterson questioned us about."

"Who was it?" Millie asked.

"Julie Bosko. She called to tell me she wanted her cabin 'deep cleaned,' whatever that means. I told her to call her room steward and she said she tried but he hadn't responded and she wanted it cleaned ASAP."

Nikki waited for several guests to pass by before continuing. "I waited to finish my shift and then stopped by Patterson's office. He jotted down a few notes but he didn't seem to think it was an odd request."

"I wonder who the room steward is," Millie mused. "I'd be curious to know what that was all about."

Nikki slowly smiled. "Isla is the room steward and I already called her. She's on her way there now to meet Julie Bosko in her cabin."

Chapter 14

Millie tapped the top of her nametag, pinned to the front of her uniform. "I'd give anything to head up there and listen in on the conversation but I'm sure the Boskos know who I am."

Annette tugged on the collar of her white chef's jacket. "I don't think I could come up with a good excuse for being there and I don't have time to change."

Millie and Annette slowly turned to Nikki.

"What?" Nikki squeaked.

Annette grabbed Nikki's hand and began dragging her down the hall. "You're the perfect person to check it out. All you have to do is tell the Boskos you're from guest services and you're stopping by to make sure Mrs. Bosko's issue was satisfactorily resolved."

Nikki pulled back. "I-I want to help, but I'm not sure about this. I don't want to get into any trouble."

"You won't." Millie hurried next to them. "Think of it as guest relations. The passenger has an issue. You're there to make sure it's been resolved."

"Right," Annette agreed. "No one will suspect a thing."

Millie's head was spinning. Roger and Delilah's suite was directly across the hall. It was late. There was no way the room steward was going to show up to clean it that late at night. Besides, if Isla were the room steward she would be busy taking care of the Bosko's issue.

Annette and Millie could hide out inside the cabin and spy on them through the peephole in the door. "We'll be there for moral support, right across the hall."

"I dunno about this." By the time they reached deck ten, Annette and Millie had managed to convince Nikki there was nothing wrong with checking up on the guests to make sure their needs were taken care of.

"The Boskos might buy it. What if Patterson shows up?" Nikki asked.

"That's a legitimate concern but you're smart. You'll think of something," Annette said.

"Well, I do have to log passenger complaints," Nikki said.

"Bingo! There you go!" Annette snapped her fingers. "You needed to investigate so you could log the issue."

As they got close to the Bosko's cabin door, Millie held a finger to her lips. She silently slid her keycard in Roger's door and Annette and she quietly slipped inside.

Annette gave Nikki a thumbs up before she closed the door.

Millie squinted her eyes and peered through the peephole. Nikki shot a quick glance in their direction and for a second, Millie thought she was going to change her mind and bolt but she didn't.

Nikki sucked in a breath and rapped on the door. The door flew open. Millie couldn't see past Nikki to see who'd answered. Nikki stepped inside the cabin and the door shut behind her.

"She's in," Millie reported as she took a step back and Annette took her place.

"What do you think it is?" Millie asked.

"It could be a toilet backup for all we know. Maybe Julie Bosko was too embarrassed to tell Nikki she flooded the cabin with toilet water."

Millie remembered the time her cousin, Liz, had done that. She still wasn't sure exactly how it had happened. The ship's plumbing system was a mystery to Millie. All she knew was when she pressed the button everything inside the toilet was sucked out.

During one of the recent staff meetings, Frank Bauer, head of maintenance, had asked Andy to remind the passengers of the ship's sensitive plumbing system. They'd been having sporadic issues with passengers flushing items they shouldn't and it was causing major headaches, not to mention a slew of passenger complaints since the clogged toilet not only affected the passenger who'd done the clogging, but an entire section of the ship that shared the same system.

"If it was a plumbing issue, I would think the Boskos would've needed to contact someone in maintenance, too," Millie pointed out.

"True." Annette shifted her feet. "Houston, we have a problem."

"What?" Millie leaned in in an attempt to look over Annette's shoulder.

"Doctor Gundervan just arrived."

"You're kidding," Millie gasped.

"I wish I was." Annette took a step back. "He went inside."

"Millie, do you copy?" Andy's voice blared from her radio and she fumbled to turn the volume down. "Uh-oh. He doesn't sound happy." Millie moved away from the door until she was certain no one in the hall could hear her talk.

"I'm here Andy. What's up?"

"I'm in Donovan's office. Can you meet me there?"

"Of course. I'm on my way." Millie's heart began to race. Those were two names she didn't want used in the same sentence...Donovan and Andy.

"That doesn't sound good," Annette said. "Would you like me to go with you?"

"Please. I can't wait to hear why I'm being summoned to Donovan's office this time of the evening." Millie retraced her steps and Annette and she eased out of the empty cabin and into the hall.

"Fifty bucks says it has something to do with the Boskos or your ex," Annette said as they picked up the pace.

"I'm sure you're right."

When they reached Donovan's office, Millie rapped lightly on the door.

Donovan opened the door and waved the women inside the room.   Not only were Donovan and Andy inside, but also Dave Patterson, Captain Armati and Staff Captain Vitale.

Donovan eased past Patterson and settled into his chair behind the desk. "I'm glad you're here too, Annette. You were next on my list."

Millie's claustrophobia threatened to kick in as her pulse began to race. Annette, noting the look on her friend's face, gave her arm an encouraging squeeze as she shifted to the side to give her a little more breathing room.

"We're waiting on Doctor Gundervan. He should be here any moment."

"I need to..." Millie was about to say she needed to step outside to get some air when there was a light rap and Doctor Gundervan stepped into the office.

"I'm sorry to call all of you here this late," Donovan apologized as the ship's doctor eased into the crowded room. "What's the report?"

"Just as we suspected," Doctor Gundervan said. "I think we have another case of norovirus on our hands."

The blood drained from Millie's face. "Norovirus?" The highly contagious virus on a cruise ship was a nightmare. Another thought entered her mind. "You said another which means there are more cases?"

Doctor Gundervan shoved his hands in his jacket pockets. "Yes. So far, we have a confirmed forty-five passengers who have come down with the illness. A few more and we'll have to implement a red alert."

"And we'll also have to report it to the CDC," Captain Armati said. He turned his attention to Gundervan. "I trust you told the guests they're not allowed to leave their cabin."

"I did." Gundervan sighed heavily. "These last two are insisting we turn the ship around to allow them to get off in San Juan."

"It's too late to turn back," Andy said. "If Isla hadn't told us about having to clean up the cabin, we never would've known the couple had contracted the virus."

"I trust we'll be adding additional sanitizers throughout the ship and station extra crew in front of the buffet and dining room to ensure passengers are using the sanitizers," Captain Vitale said.

"Of course. After we leave here, I'll call a meeting with my staff to give them a heads up and ask them to keep an eye out," Andy promised.

Donovan turned to Annette. "Please meet with your kitchen staff to give them a heads up. We may need to station some of them in front of the dining areas." He shuffled the papers on his desk. "I'll let you know if anything changes." It was his way of dismissing the group and they slowly started to shuffle out of the room.

Millie tugged on Gundervan's arm and asked him to stay behind for a moment. "Is it possible Delilah Osborne wasn't poisoned after all and perhaps fell ill from a severe case of norovirus?"

"I've already considered that angle." Doctor Gundervan shook his head. "As much as I would like to say it was, the woman had a lethal reaction to nuts. Patterson is sending the food to a lab for a thorough analysis, but I noted a lingering odor of peanut butter on the cream puff." He shifted his gaze to Donovan, "I'm surprised if the woman had that level of sensitivity, she didn't smell the peanut butter before eating the food."

He walked Millie to the door. "It has been a long day. I'm going to turn in for the night but will have my radio turned down low and next to my bed in case we have another call come in."

Millie followed the weary doctor out of Donovan's office. "We had such a quiet few months while you were gone, Millie."

"I heard. I'm only sorry it hasn't been smooth sailing for at least a few more days," Millie said.

The doctor headed toward the bank of elevators and Millie headed in the opposite direction when she caught a glimpse of Nikki and Annette huddled close together and off to the side. She made her way over to them.

"I was telling Annette Mrs. Bosko let me into the room before she collapsed in the chair. She kept saying the same thing over and over, that they never should've come on the cruise."

"Did she say why?" Millie asked.

"She said she hated the ship, hated cruising and the only reason she'd come was because Delilah Osborne had begged her. She said she couldn't stand Roger, couldn't stand Delilah's daughter, Linda. The only reason she'd agreed to come was because Delilah had told her friend someone was harassing her and she was scared."

"Harassing her before she got on the ship?" Annette asked.

"Right."

"Did she tell Patterson that when he talked to her?" Surely, the woman would've mentioned it when Patterson questioned her.

"I tried to ask her but she started heaving..."

Millie held up a hand. "I get the picture. Why would someone be harassing her? Beth never mentioned anything about it. Roger must've known." *Unless Roger was behind it.* Maybe

Delilah feared Roger, but then why would she move forward with plans to marry him?

"I don't know." Nikki shook her head. "I hope I'm not going to come down with norovirus now!"

"As long as you didn't touch anything inside their cabin and you washed your hands right after, you should be okay." Millie patted her arm. "You were a huge help, Nikki. I owe you one."

"Thanks Millie."

Annette and Millie told Nikki goodnight and then made their way past the elevators to the stairs.

"I smell a rat," Annette said.

"It seems like there was a lot of bad blood swirling around Delilah."

When they reached the crew deck, Millie paused. "I'm going to try to jot out a timeline of events. Maybe it will help clear my head and something will jump out at me. Thanks for the backup."

"You're welcome." Annette smiled. "I know you'd do the same for me."

Millie wandered down the hall to her cabin. Danielle was nowhere in sight so Millie got ready for bed before she settled into the chair in front of the desk. She reached for the notepad and pen on top but when she spotted her worn Bible, she grabbed it instead.

She flipped the Bible open to where she'd left off. Millie was studying the Book of Isaiah, one of her favorites for reading Biblical prophecies and turned to Isaiah, Chapter 41:

"So do not fear, for I am with you; do not be dismayed, for I am your God.

I will strengthen you and help you; I will uphold you with my righteous right hand."
Isaiah 41:10 NIV

Millie closed her eyes and meditated on the words. It seemed as if she hadn't had a moment's peace since boarding the ship. There were times she wondered if she was meant to be there and perhaps somehow God was trying to tell her something.

She finished reading chapter 41 before tucking her bookmarker inside. Millie closed her eyes to pray. She'd been so wrapped up in all that was going on, that her prayer life had suffered.

Millie asked God to forgive her and then poured her heart out, questioning her reason for being on the ship and questioning why it seemed she had a dark cloud of disaster following her around.

A sense of peace enveloped her and by the time she lifted her head, she felt much better. She glanced at the pad of paper and pen and then slid them to the corner. She would have plenty of time to work on a timeline in the morning.

All she wanted to do at that moment was spend a few hours stress and drama-free. She crawled into bed and pulled the covers around her chin before falling asleep.

Chapter 15

Millie woke to Danielle shuffling around inside the cabin. She opened her eyes and blinked in an attempt to adjust to the bright fluorescent light. "What are you doing?"

She watched as Danielle, who was already dressed in her work uniform, flipped the light on and then stood in front of the full-length mirror, deftly smoothing her long blonde hair into a ponytail.

"I'm scheduled to work in the library for a few hours."

Millie narrowed her eyes as she gazed at Danielle suspiciously. "You hate the library. In fact, you hate reading."

"It was either that or host the singles early bird paint and pastries get-together."

Millie threw her covers back and swung her legs over the side of the bed. "Do you really hate hosting the singles events that much? We can ask Andy to start swapping some of our schedules so you can get a break."

"I have to admit there are times I get tired of the singles events, but it's not that. I was looking forward to the painting get-together, but there's this creepy guy who keeps hitting on me at the singles events and I'm trying to shake him." Danielle tugged on the bottom of her blouse.

"I'm not surprised." Millie slowly stood and lifted her hands over her head to stretch. "I'm surprised it doesn't happen more, Danielle. You're one hot chick."

Danielle snorted. "Thanks, I think. I've been hit on a few times and have had to nip some advances in the bud but this guy won't give up and he's starting to get on my nerves. I'm afraid I'm gonna get fed up and deck him."

"What does he look like?" Millie wondered if she'd seen him around the ship.

"About yay tall." Danielle held her hand level to her chin. He's got bulging eyes, a spreading rotunda and when he gets close, his breath smells like curdled milk and he talks like this." Danielle blew a burst of air from her mouth. "Mark-uh."

"His name is Mark?"

"Yah, at least I think it's Mark. I had better head out before I'm late. Buh-bye," she gasped.

Millie grinned as Danielle slipped out of their cabin to start her shift in the library.

With everything that had gone on the previous evening, Millie had forgotten to stop by Andy's office to grab her schedule. It was still early and she had plenty of time to head down there to pick it up.

Andy wasn't there but the schedule was lying on his conference table. She picked it up and slipped her reading glasses on. She scanned the list and paused when she noticed *Cruise Clue*, the new adult mystery/scavenger hunt, scheduled for early afternoon.

There was also a white envelope with her name on it. Millie reached inside and removed the contents. Clipped together were small slips of paper. Each clipped pile was numbered. She scanned the instructions and after realizing these were the clues for the game, she tucked the papers in her jacket pocket and headed out.

Thankfully, she wasn't scheduled to co-host one of the early morning exercise classes which gave her enough time to grab a bagel and cream cheese before heading to the theater for the St. Thomas port stop shopping talk. St. Thomas was famous for jewelry and the fact passengers could purchase duty-free merchandise on the island was a big draw.

Millie was hosting the event. Because of her recent break, she'd forgotten some of the key tips so she skimmed through her notes before stepping onto the stage to start the presentation. After the slide show ended, many of the passengers made their way to the front to pick up discount coupon books.

The theater emptied and Millie headed to the library to check on Danielle, concerned for her friend now that she was aware a passenger on board was making her uncomfortable.

She stepped inside the small library where several clusters of passengers sat at tables playing board games and cards while others lounged in leather chairs near the large picture windows.

Millie spotted Danielle sitting at a small desk near the door. "Have you had any sightings of your overzealous admirer?"

Danielle tightened her ponytail. "No thank goodness. Maybe he found someone else to stalk." The two women chatted for several moments before Danielle's replacement wandered in and the women exited the library.

"Have you heard anything else on the norovirus?" Danielle whispered as they walked.

"No." The last thing Millie needed was to catch the virus. She had enough on her plate to deal with. "Maybe that's what happened to your mysterious admirer."

The women passed by the buffet as they made their way to the salad bar, located in the center of the dining room.

Millie spread a thick layer of iceberg lettuce on the bottom of her plate. She topped it with tomatoes, onions, cheddar cheese, and green peppers. Her final stop was to add a large scoop of ranch dressing and croutons before she followed Danielle to a table in the corner.

Danielle slid into the chair across from Millie. "I was thinking the same thing. Norovirus is bad news." She spread her napkin on her lap and reached for her fork. "So you've given up on figuring out how Delilah ended up eating the tainted cream puff."

"There's not much else I can do. I've reached a standstill. The suspects are now off the ship, with the exception of the Boskos, who are in quarantine since they're contagious."

They discussed the possibility of both Roger and Dixie Keebler following through on their threats to sue the cruise line before moving on to more pleasant topics.

Millie told Danielle she'd enjoyed her time at home but all the time she'd been there, she wondered what was happening aboard Siren of the Seas.

"And you were wondering what Captain Armati was doing," Danielle teased.

"True. I missed him, I missed everyone, even you," Millie joked.

They finished their salads and strolled across the pool area to the other end. A somber faced Dave Patterson and Andy were coming from the other direction.

A chill ran up Millie's spine as her eyes met Andy's eyes. Something told her the serious expression involved her and a knot formed in the pit of her stomach. "What happened?"

Her first thought was something had happened to one of her children or to Captain Armati.

"The corporate office in Miami just called," Donovan said in a low voice as several passengers strolled by. "Let's talk over here."

The four of them headed to a quiet corner, right behind the towel cart and out of the main thoroughfare.

"They received a formal complaint from Roger E. Sanders, accusing Siren of the Seas and Majestic Cruise lines of negligence in the death of Delilah Osborne."

Millie's hand flew to her mouth. "He's not even home yet."

"He didn't waste any time," Andy grimaced.

"That's not all," Donovan said. "He specifically named you."

"Me?" Millie squeaked. Beth had warned her Roger was on the warpath and was spouting threats and accusations Millie was somehow responsible for Delilah's death, but she didn't think he seriously believed Millie was somehow involved. "That's absurd."

"Now what?" Danielle asked.

Andy sucked in a deep breath. "Patterson already closed the investigation and filed the paperwork. Corporate is forcing him to reopen it. He wants you to stop by his office as soon as possible."

"I'm on my way," Millie said. She turned to go and Andy grabbed her arm.

"We know you're innocent Millie. This is a formality, but if you can think of anything, anything at all your daughter may have said, please be sure to let Patterson know."

"I will," Millie promised. She left the three standing on the deck and marched down the steps. "Unbelievable," Millie hissed under her breath. The more she stomped, the angrier she became.

If the whole matter weren't so serious and tragic for Delilah and her family, it would've made a great soap opera. Who would believe an assistant cruise director's ex-husband would bring his bride-to-be on board the ship where she worked and ask the captain of the ship, who also happened to be the cruise director's boyfriend, to marry them and then have the woman die after eating peanuts or peanut butter?

Millie wasn't sure whom to blame. She wanted to place the blame squarely on Roger's shoulders. At best, it was an accident, pure and simple. At worst, it was a sinister crime, carried out by someone close to Delilah, someone who knew she was deathly allergic to peanuts and somehow managed to trick her into eating the poisonous food.

Dave Patterson's office was dark but Millie decided to knock anyway. When he didn't answer, she turned around and retraced her steps.

She could feel her blood pressure rise and knew she'd reached a point where she was about to blow her cool so she headed back to her cabin to cool down.

She stayed inside for several moments and when she spied her cell phone on the counter, she picked it up. Millie rarely used her cell phone while the ship was in open water, partly because reception was hit or miss and partly because the roaming fees and service provider charges were ridiculously expensive.

She picked up the phone and switched it on. There was a text message from Beth. Her daughter had sent several family pictures she'd taken during the cruise and Millie smiled as she gazed at her beautiful family. Looking at the pictures calmed Millie and helped put things into perspective.

She flipped through the photos and frowned when she spotted a group photo, one with Delilah, Roger, Linda, Delilah's daughter, as well as a man Millie didn't recognize. She assumed the man was Linda's husband.

The group photo was the last one Beth had sent so Millie switched her cell phone off and slipped it into her jacket pocket before she left the cabin and headed for an open deck where she hoped she'd be able to get enough bars on her cell phone to dial out.

She plucked the phone from her pocket and switched it on. There were three bars, enough to dial out so Millie quickly pressed her daughter's cell phone number.

The call went right to voice mail and Millie, not wanting to cause Beth more stress, thanked her for sending the pictures and told her she'd call her when she reached St. Croix before switching the phone off and slipping it back inside her pocket.

The Cruise Clue mystery/scavenger hunt was next on Millie's list of scheduled activities and she forced herself to focus on the task at hand.

The sun deck's tiki bar was the listed meeting place and Millie hurried over to the bar, not far from the mini golf course. The bar area was packed and she quickly realized the passengers were all there to play the game.

Andy had only given her enough packets for five teams so Millie had to double the number of people per group and then randomly select "team captains." She was relieved Andy had given her detailed instructions including giving each of the teams five minutes to go over the clues and talk strategy.

While one of the teams decided a "divide and conquer" plan would work best, others opted to work the clues in reverse.

The final group's strategy was to skip going over a game plan and get a jump-start on the game as they split up and canvassed the ship, searching for clues.

According to the instructions, each team was given approximately one hour to either take pictures of, or bring back as many of the items as possible. The team that arrived back to the bar area first with the most items/clues uncovered, would win. Any team who arrived late, even by a minute was automatically disqualified.

After the teams left, Millie hopped onto a stool in front of the tiki bar and ordered a Diet Coke. She pulled out the game's instruction sheet, which listed both the clues and answers. She placed a hand over the answers and worked her way down the list as she tried to guess what they were.

"Whatcha' doing?" Annette pulled out the bar stool next to Millie and plopped down.

"What are you doing?" Millie peered at her friend over the top of her reading glasses.

"Looking for you. I have a couple hours off and wondered if you were having a better day today."

"No, I'm not," Millie said bluntly. "Donovan tracked me down to let me know Roger filed a complaint at corporate and named me in the complaint."

"Whew!" Annette rolled her eyes. "What a jerk."

"I realize he's in shock, in mourning, or whatever, but surely he knows deep down I didn't kill Delilah."

"Maybe in his mind, he thinks you did do it, that you only planned to make her sick, not kill her but it went too far and she died," Annette theorized. "Did you get a chance to jot down any notes?"

"No. After I got back to the cabin last night, I read my Bible and went to bed." Millie glanced at her watch. "I have some extra time right now while I wait for the passengers to get back here from the scavenger hunt."

"No time like the present," Annette quipped. "I can try to help."

Millie flipped the game's answer sheet over and scribbled "suspects" at the top of the sheet. "You're good at this. Who do you think may have intentionally poisoned Delilah?"

"Roger, her sister, her brother-in-law, her daughter, son-in-law and the friends," Annette rattled off.

"Which is everyone."

"Exactly. We can't rule anyone out. Supposing it wasn't an accident. Supposing you didn't do it."

Millie interrupted. "Of course I didn't do it."

"See? We're already eliminating suspects," Annette joked. "In all seriousness, what do we know?"

"We know Delilah ordered room service. The Boskos, across the hall, ordered around the same time. Carmen delivered the food. Roger left to get sodas. When he came back, Delilah was lying on the floor, clutching her throat and the tainted cream puff, and that her throat had swollen shut, suffocating her."

"We also know Delilah's balcony connected with her sister's balcony on one side and her daughter's balcony on the other."

"Yep and there was no connecting interior door."

"We've also concluded it's possible that while Carmen was delivering other room service orders, someone snuck into the service area, spied the ticket on top of Delilah's order and smeared some peanut butter on the food."

Millie wrinkled her nose. "That's a stretch."

231

"What can I get you Miss Annette?" Dario, one of the bartenders and Millie's friend, stepped close.

"It's been a long day. Give me an eggnog, make it a double."

Dario's eyes widened.

"I'm kidding. I'll take a ginger ale." She turned to Millie. "Think about your conversation with Delilah the other day when she confronted you about selling your house. Did she say anything that struck you as odd or unusual?"

"No." Millie shook her head. "She took me by surprise. I was shocked she was standing there in an area where passengers are not allowed."

"Unless you're one of the younger crewmembers and you hook up with one of the passengers, but that's neither here nor there. Go on."

"She said she and Roger wanted to move and she was interested in buying my house because of the lake view." Millie subconsciously clenched her fist. "She wanted to buy it, tear it down and build a new one."

Annette interrupted. "She sounds like a wacko. She steals your husband, flaunts him in your face and then she wants to buy your house just to tear it down."

"Right?"

"Go on. I didn't meant to interrupt." Annette popped the tab on her can of ginger ale and took a big swig.

"She said she and Roger needed a bigger house because she thought her daughter was going to move in with them."

"The daughter who was on the ship?"

"I dunno." Millie shook her head. "She may have more than one daughter."

Millie sipped her Diet Coke. "I told her no and I guess our voices got a little loud because Tariq stopped and asked if I needed help. I escorted Delilah out of the crew area right after that."

"You never saw her again?"

"Nope. The next morning Patterson tracked me down to tell me she was dead."

Millie twirled her straw in her glass. "The Boskos seem suspect. They are odd ducks, not real friendly and the fact they stayed on the ship and decided to finish the cruise after their 'close' friend died strikes me as odd."

"Maybe we should trail 'em for a while. You know, track their moves."

"Remember they came down with norovirus," Millie pointed out. "They've been confined to their cabin until further notice."

"You're right. I forgot. I guess that eliminates a search of their cabin. The place is probably full of cooties."

A group of passengers hurried toward them. "My contestants," Millie whispered.

"I'm outta here." Annette gulped the rest of her ginger ale and hopped off the barstool. "Stop by later. We gotta get you out of the frying pan, my friend."

Millie watched Annette walk across the deck. "I sure do hope we can."

Chapter 16

After the scavenger hunt wrapped up, Millie headed toward Andy's office to check in. It was late afternoon and Millie was beginning to fade. She passed by the sushi bar and paused. She'd never been a huge fan of what she'd secretly nicknamed "squishy."

Annette had attempted to get Millie to try it but none of it sounded appetizing.

A kitchen staff member, someone Millie knew but for the life of her couldn't remember the man's name, smiled. "You like to try?"

She took a step closer and studied the offerings. Millie pointed at a small black bowl of soup with chunks of green floating around inside. "What's that?"

"Miso soup. You want to try it?" The staff member slid a napkin and small tasting spoon toward Millie. "It has green onion and is very good."

Millie scooped up the soup, the spoon and the napkin and stepped to the side to let the guests behind her reach the counter. "Thank you."

She dipped her small spoon in the soup and tasted the warm salty concoction. It was good. She quickly finished the small sampler and handed the man behind the counter her empty bowl and dirty spoon. "You're right. It was very tasty."

"You try sushi?" Millie didn't have the heart to tell him no, so she took the napkin and rolled rice piece. "Thank you. I better get back to work."

Millie covered the sushi with the napkin and made her way into the hall as she searched for the nearest trash bin but couldn't find one so she headed to Andy's office still carrying the bite size sample.

Danielle and Andy were both inside and looked up when she made her way into the office. "I brought you a surprise."

Danielle loved sushi. "Yum! What kind is it?"

"I have no idea." Millie wrinkled her nose.

Danielle nibbled the treat while Millie told Andy the scavenger hunt had been a huge success.

"I haven't scheduled anyone for Killer Karaoke tonight." Andy tapped his pen on top of the desk.

"I'll do it," Danielle said. "I've never done it before."

Andy hesitated.

"I say let her host it," Millie said. "It's only fair. What am I going to host?"

"The Mix and Mingle singles party."

Millie groaned. "Is there time to change my mind?"

"No way!" Danielle chuckled.

"I'm kidding." Millie patted Danielle's arm. "Speaking of singles, has your stalker/admirer shown up again?"

"No, thank goodness."

Andy leaned forward in his chair. "What stalker?"

Danielle explained how a passenger had been a little too "friendly" and she'd had to put him in his place. She attempted to assure Andy she had it under control. "I think I scared him off. I haven't seen him all day."

Despite Danielle's reassurance she had it under control, Millie could tell Andy was concerned. He turned to Millie. "I'm going to put you in charge of hosting Mix and Mingle until further notice."

"Aye-aye sir." Millie gave Andy a small salute. "I guess I better run over there to set up the munchie station and make sure we've got some decent music ready to rock the place. Hopefully they don't boo me out of there."

"You'll do fine." Andy walked the women to the office door. He turned to Danielle. "You, young lady, need to let me know if this passenger approaches you again."

"Thanks Dad," Danielle gave Andy a quick hug and slipped out of the office.

"I'll try to keep an eye on her," Millie promised. She followed Danielle out of the office and by the time she reached the outer hall, Danielle was long gone.

No one matching Danielle's description of "Mark" showed up for the singles event and Millie was surprised by how much fun she had hosting the event. It was a lively group and a nice mix of younger and older guests.

Millie's hosting events ended when she finished emceeing the Gem of the Seas, the headliner show. Afterwards, she wandered to the atrium to watch Danielle host Killer Karaoke and she caught Millie's eye at one point while one of the young guests on board was singing a rousing rendition of "Blue Skies." She gave Millie a thumbs up.

Millie finished making her rounds and by the time she tromped back to her cabin, she was exhausted. Tomorrow was the St. Croix port day and a wave of sadness washed over Millie as she thought about her family and how they'd all been looking forward to visiting Buck Island.

She quickly pushed the melancholy mood aside. Millie had bigger problems to deal with, namely Roger formally accusing her of being involved in Delilah's death. She needed to suck it up and move on. She wasn't even sure if she had the energy to worry about what Roger might or might not do.

Danielle wandered into the cabin as Millie finished getting ready for bed.

"Great job on Killer Karaoke," Millie complimented. "The crowd enjoyed it."

"I did too." Danielle smiled, the dimple in her cheek deepening. "It's too bad I can't host it more often. How did the Mix and Mingle party go?"

"Great." Millie removed her hair clip and ran her fingers through her hair. "I think I had as much fun as you did. We should ask Andy if he'll let us swap events for the time being. You take Killer Karaoke and I'll do at least one of the Mix and Mingle parties."

"Really?" Danielle bounced on her toes. "Are you sure? I mean, I don't want to take over one of your favorite jobs."

"I'm sure, Danielle. Besides, it's good for us to swap jobs every so often."

"Cool." Danielle reached inside her closet for her pajamas. "What are you doing tomorrow?"

"I was going to go to Buck Island with my family." Millie attempted to keep her tone light but Danielle could tell she was upset.

"Why don't you invite Captain Armati on a date? You haven't spent much time with him since you got back on board," Danielle suggested.

"I hadn't thought of that. I've always let him be the one to invite me. Maybe I should."

It didn't take much for Danielle to convince Millie to invite the captain and before she could change her mind, she picked up the phone handset and dialed his private line. She was surprised when he answered and Danielle slipped into the bathroom to give them some privacy.

"Hello Millie," Captain Armati's deep voice echoed through the phone. "I've been trying to reach you on your radio."

"You have?" Millie reached for her radio to check the volume. "I've had it on all night but now that you mention it, it's been very quiet."

"Perhaps the batteries have died," the captain said. "I know you planned to spend the day with your family in St. Croix but now that they're gone, I have some free time tomorrow and thought you might like to spend part of your day with me instead."

"I would love to." She reached up to touch the necklace the captain had given her before she left on leave.

"Great. I've already taken the liberty of planning a surprise in the hopes you would say yes."

"What kind of surprise?"

"You'll have to wait and see. No need to bring anything with you except your sunglasses and a camera."

They agreed on a meeting time near the gangway.

Danielle emerged from the bathroom, noted the glow in Millie's eyes and smiled. "Ah, I see you have a date tomorrow."

"Yeah. I think the batteries in my radio are dead. Captain Armati has been trying to reach me. He's taking me somewhere tomorrow and says it's a surprise."

"Oh." Danielle clapped her hands. "I love surprises."

"Me too. Sometimes. He said all I need to bring with me are my sunglasses and my phone to take pictures."

"I wish I had someone to hang out with," Danielle said.

"What about what's-his-name Lorenzo, the guy who transferred from Marquise of the Seas?"

"He's a womanizer," Danielle climbed the ladder to the top bunk. "And a jerk."

Millie waited until Danielle had settled in under the covers before turning off the light. "There are plenty of other fish in the sea."

It was quiet for a long moment before Danielle's soft voice filled the cabin. "Thanks Millie."

"For what?"

"For being like a mom and worrying about me. I don't have anyone anymore, not since Casey died."

"You're like a daughter to me, Danielle," Millie whispered and then offered a silent prayer for her young friend.

Danielle had been very tight-lipped about her brother, Casey. The only thing Millie knew was Casey had been Danielle's younger brother and Danielle blamed herself for his death.

Millie wasn't even sure if Danielle had family back home, wherever "home" was. Judging by the comment about Millie being like a mother, she had a sneaky suspicion her young cabin mate had no immediate family, at least none she was close to.

"Whenever you're ready to talk Danielle, I'm here."

"I know," Danielle whispered back. "Goodnight Millie."

Millie knew the conversation was over and as Millie closed her eyes, she prayed for Danielle again, for the deep hurt she knew was just below the surface she tried so hard to hide from everyone. She also prayed for Delilah's family, for Roger and that Delilah's death would be put to rest.

Millie wasn't sure how long she tossed and turned before finally drifting off to sleep. She didn't wake until she felt the gentle vibration of the ship as it docked on the island.

She could hear Danielle stirring as the vibration increased and Millie slipped out of her bunkbed. The captain, Nic, had told her to meet him near the gangway around eleven, which would work out perfectly since Millie was assisting Andy near the gangway to see the first wave of passengers disembarking for a day of fun and sun on the small island.

She made it there right after the crew slid the exit ramp into place and passengers began disembarking.

Andy waited for a lull in the crowd before turning to Millie. "Are you getting off today?" He knew Millie had planned to spend the day with her family.

"Yes," Millie nodded.

"Are you heading to town or the beach with Annette and Cat?"

"No." Millie shook her head and Andy raised a brow. "Ah. I see. The captain was trying to reach you yesterday."

Millie interrupted. "Which reminds me, I think the batteries in my radio are dead. I'll replace them before I leave the ship."

"So where is the captain taking you?" The island was small. Most of the activities involved outdoor excursions...snorkeling, scuba diving. There was also a botanical garden and small fort.

"It's a surprise." A group of passengers approached to ask if it was safe to drink the water or eat the food on the island. Andy answered their questions and then waited until they were out of earshot.

"I hope you have a wonderful day off, Millie," Andy said. "You deserve it after all that's gone on." He changed the subject. "How did the Mix and Mingle singles party go?"

"It was fun. I enjoyed it much more than I thought I would. If you don't mind, Danielle and I would like to swap for the time being. I can host one of the Mix and Mingle parties and she'll host Killer Karaoke."

Andy nodded thoughtfully. "Okay. Agreed. It's good to switch things up and learn each other's jobs." He glanced at his watch. "What time are you meeting the captain?"

"Eleven."

"You better get a move on. I can manage on my own."

Millie thanked Andy before making her way downstairs. She stopped by the maintenance office to grab some new batteries for her radio before heading to the cabin to get ready for her date.

It had been a long time since Nic and she had spent any time alone together, and Millie primped in the bathroom as long as she dared. She slipped a swimsuit on under a pair of shorts and sleeveless blouse, stuck her feet in a new pair of sandals she'd bought back home and then hurried to the gangway.

She hovered off to the side to wait. A short time later Nic emerged from the elevator wearing swim trunks, a t-shirt with the ship's logo on the front and a ball cap. He was also wearing a backpack, carrying a large bag in one hand and Scout's dog carrier in his other.

Millie hurried over to take the carrier. Scout was so excited to see Millie that he began to paw at the metal bars. She stuck her fingers inside the cage and rubbed Scout's head. "Aw. You get to come with us, too?"

Millie lifted the cage so it was close to her face. "Are you going to tell me where we're going?"

Woof!

"That's what I thought. You've been sworn to secrecy," Millie joked.

Nic smiled. "Scout…a man's most loyal companion and keeper of all secrets." He shifted the large bag to his other hand. "Are you ready to go?"

Millie nodded. "As ready as I'll ever be."

Chapter 17

Nic and Millie stepped down the gangway. Several of the crew who had worked on board Siren of the Seas for many moons, recognized the captain and gave him a small salute. One of them winked at Millie and she grinned. Despite his best attempt to remain incognito, the beloved captain carried an air of authority that was hard to miss.

Nic reached for Millie's free hand. "This way my dear." He led her to the nearby marina and a small boat, the Sea Vixen, tied up at the dock.

"Captain Armati?" A tall thin man aboard the boat stepped forward.

"Meeko?" the captain asked as he handed the man the bag he'd refused to let Millie touch and then climbed on the boat.

"Yes sir." The man took Scout's carrier from Millie and handed him off to Nic, who gently eased the carrier onto the floor near the back.

Nic returned to the front of the boat to help Millie. After they were both safely on board, they settled onto the bench seat in the back and sat close together.

Millie slid her sunglasses on as the boat slipped away from the dock and turned toward open water.

Siren of the Seas was the only ship in port and Millie studied the massive cruise ship. She loved to see the ship from a different perspective. It seemed so much bigger on the outside.

Nic squeezed Millie's hand. "You miss her already?"

"No." Millie smiled. "I'm appreciating the sheer size of her. She's a beaut."

The conversation shifted to the island. Captain Armati shared a story of the time he'd snorkeled on the island some years back. A pod of dolphins had shown up and they surrounded the snorkelers as they played in the water nearby.

Millie had seen a few dolphins some time back, but never up close. "That would be awesome." The boat slowed.

"We are here," Meeko announced. He cut the engine and the boat drifted to shore. "This is as close as I can get."

"Perfect." The captain stood and made his way to the bow of the boat before he slid off the front and into the crystal-clear water. He reached for the secret bag. "I'll be right back."

Nic waded to shore, placed the large bag on top of a nearby rock and then waded back out to the boat.

Millie carried Scout's carrier as she eased her way to the front. She handed Scout to the captain before she removed her sandals and held them in one hand. She followed Nic's lead as she slid off the front and grasped the hand he held out.

"I will be back at 2:30," Meeko said before starting the boat's motor.

"Perfect." Nic handed Millie Scout's carrier and then used his free hand to push the front of the boat out into deeper water. They watched as Meeko turned the small vessel around and began the short trip back to the mainland.

Millie glanced down into the water and gasped as colorful tropical fish swarmed around her legs.

"Stay here. I'll be right back." Nic waded to shore and set Scout's carrier near the large bag before he returned to where Millie was waiting. He turned around and pointed to the backpack he was still wearing. "There's a box of cornflakes in the front pocket."

Millie unzipped the front pocket and pulled out the small box of cereal before handing it to Nic. "What is this for?"

"We're going to feed the fish." Nic opened the top of the box and peeled back the plastic liner. "Hold out your hand."

Millie held out her hand and he dumped a small mound into her palm. "Now we feed the fish."

Millie bent forward and gazed into the turquoise water. She sprinkled the corn flakes on top of the water and moments later, a school of fish appeared. Some were a vivid blue with black splotches, others a turquoise and yellow color while still others were brown and white striped. Spikes stuck out along the top of the brown and white fish. There were also spikes surrounding the fins.

She dipped the tips of her fingers in the warm water, certain that if she reached down a few more inches, she could touch them.

They finished emptying the box of cereal and waded to shore where Nic picked up the mysterious bag while Millie opened the door to Scout's carrier.

The pint size pup darted out of the carrier and onto the sand. He pranced in circles and Millie could almost see the smile on his face as he savored his freedom and began running along the shoreline. "He loves it."

Scout sprinted ahead and Nic had to chase after him. He reached inside Scout's carrier and pulled out his leash. "He loves it a little too much."

Nic clipped the leash to Scout's collar and then shut the door to the empty carrier. "We can leave this here. I'm sure no one will bother it."

"We don't have far to go." Nic reached for Millie's hand and the three of them meandered along the shoreline. Millie drank in the tranquility of the small island. There wasn't another soul in sight.

A gentle breeze tossed Millie's hair and the bright Caribbean sun warmed her face. She breathed deeply and could feel the tension leave her body. She wished she could capture the moment and bottle it for all of the times when life's stresses overwhelmed her.

"We're here." Nic stopped abruptly. He pointed at a secluded cove surrounded by large rocks. It formed a horseshoe shape. He set the bag on top of a nearby boulder, reached inside and pulled out a checkered flannel blanket.

He handed her one end of the blanket and they spread it out on the sandy beach while Scout attempted to hop on the blanket they were trying to unfold.

"You're such a stinker." Millie scooped him up in her arms and held him close before setting him on the sand so they could finish smoothing out the blanket.

Nic reached inside the secret bag and pulled out a soft side cooler, set it on the blanket and then pulled out a second cooler.

"We're having a..."

"Picnic," Nic finished her sentence.

"This is perfect," Millie gushed. She watched as he pulled out a small plastic bin. Inside one bin was an array of fresh fruit...grapes, pineapple wedges, chunks of juicy watermelon along with strawberries and blueberries.

Inside another container were chicken salad wraps. There was also a zip-lock bag with packets of ranch dressing, mayonnaise and mustard. Nic pulled out two more containers and set them next to the wraps. "We also have some potato salad and coleslaw."

There was one last container, full of small chunks of chicken and beef. "Scout's lunch," Nic explained. He set the pup's food off to one side.

After the spread of delicious food was arranged on the blanket, the two of them settled in to enjoy their feast while Scout ran over the top of their legs, turning them into a mini obstacle course.

Millie reached out and patted his head. "You
don't know what to do with yourself, do you?"

Scout licked Millie's hand and finally settled
onto her lap.

"Let's pray." Nic took Millie's hand and they
bowed their heads. "Dear Lord. Thank you for
this food. Thank you for this wonderful woman I
love with all my heart. Thank you for bringing
her into my life. May you bless our lives from
this day forward."

Nic's prayer brought sudden tears to Millie's
eyes and she blinked them back as she lifted her
head. "That was beautiful. Thank you." She
wiped away a tear that trickled down her cheek.

It had been a long few days, a long few months
even. She had missed him while she was in
Michigan, and although they had talked on the
phone whenever he was in port, it wasn't the
same.

"Before we start eating." Nic stuck his hand inside his pants pocket as he shifted to his knees. "I'd like to ask you something."

Chapter 18

Millie's heart leapt into her throat as it dawned on her what was happening. She clamped her hand across her mouth and her eyes widened as she stared at the box Nic held out.

"Millie, will you marry me? Will you be my wife?"

"I..." Her eyes darted from Nic's face to the ring and back again. She began to feel lightheaded as she tried to grasp what he was saying.

"I hope that's a yes."

"Yes," Millie whispered.

Nic tugged the round diamond solitaire from the center of the small box. "May I?" He motioned to Millie's hand.

Millie's hand trembled as she held it out and Nic slipped the ring on her finger. She burst into tears as she stared at the ring.

"I hope those are happy tears."

Scout let out a small yelp as Millie flung herself into the arms of the man she had grown to love, who had stood by her during the last year, who had been her rock, her constant in a world of chaos.

"Yes, yes, yes!" Millie chanted as Nic held her in his arms.

They stayed locked in an embrace until Nic slowly pulled back, his eyes gazing deeply into hers. He leaned forward and Millie tilted her head.

The kiss started out slow but quickly deepened as Millie threw caution to the wind and promised Nic in that moment a lifetime of love, giving her heart freely to him.

Millie wanted the moment, the kiss to last forever as time stood still.

Scout interrupted their intimate moment as he latched onto the bottom of Millie's blouse and began tugging.

Millie smiled in the kiss and reluctantly pulled back. "Someone is jealous."

Nic grinned and rubbed one of his pup's ears. "You weren't supposed to do that." He leaned back. "I suppose it's best. We don't want to get carried away."

"Or do we," Millie flirted. She reached for Scout's container of food. "We better feed Scout first."

Nic handed Millie a paper napkin. She unfolded the napkin and placed it near the edge of the blanket before dumping Scout's lunch in the center.

The diamond caught Millie's eye as the sun reflected off the large stone. She lifted her hand to admire the ring. "When...how?"

Nic opened the container of fruit and reached for a strawberry. "I ordered the ring right after you left the ship to head home for your break. I've had it in my dresser drawer for some time now. I couldn't wait for you to come back to propose."

He went on. "I planned to bring you here to Buck Island. I had it all planned; the perfect romantic beach proposal. When I found out your daughter and family were coming and you booked a beach day with them, my plan was to postpone it until next week, after I met them. It would have been the perfect opportunity to let your daughter know of my plans but fate had a different idea."

"Delilah," Millie said.

"Yes," Nic said. "After discovering your ex-husband and his fiancée were on board and pressed me to marry them, I decided perhaps it was best to wait until they were off the ship and the dust settled."

"You didn't want their marriage to mar our engagement," Millie guessed.

Nic nodded. "After Delilah's death and the recent events, I decided to chat with Beth and her husband to get their thoughts. They gave me their blessing and at Beth's prompting, I decided to go ahead and propose."

Millie's eyes widened. "My daughter knows?"

"Yes, she does and I promised her as soon as we returned to St. Croix this afternoon, I would have you call her." Nic reached for Millie's hand. "You have a lovely family and I can't wait to be a bigger part of your life."

"That stinker," Millie said. "I had no idea. I'm sure she's bursting at the seams."

Scout finished nibbling on his lunch and decided to explore the picnic area as he dragged his leash across the blanket and onto the sand.

Millie grabbed the leash and looped the end around Nic's backpack. The leash was long enough for Scout to dip the tips of his paws in the water and he wandered back and forth, sniffing the air.

"The sand and waves must feel strange to him," Millie observed.

"I feel guilty for leaving him on the ship so much of the time and decided to take him ashore with me, with us, as much as possible."

A tingle ran through Millie at the word "us." It would take some getting used to. She'd finally grown comfortable with living alone, if you could call sharing a small cabin with Danielle "alone."

"We should eat," Nic urged as he handed Millie a plate.

Millie placed one of the chicken wraps on the side of her plate, added a spoonful of potato salad and coleslaw and then scooped a heaping mound of fresh fruit on the edge.

It dawned on her she'd skipped breakfast. The fresh air and sunshine had made her hungry. She inhaled the first half of her wrap and all of her potato salad before noticing Nic was eating much slower. "Oh my! I didn't realize I was so hungry."

"I'm savoring the wonderful company of my bride-to-be." Nic took a bite of his wrap and set the uneaten piece on his plate. "We have a lot of decisions to make."

They discussed a wedding date and decided the sooner the better but they both wanted to give their children enough time to adjust to the idea their parents were getting remarried and to make travel arrangements.

They considered an island wedding and although Millie thought it would be romantic and beautiful, they quickly agreed a neutral spot where Nic's daughter, Fiona, and her family as well as Beth and family, Millie's son, Blake, along with his girlfriend, could easily reach.

Miami would be the perfect spot for all and they decided to pick the date as soon as they shared the good news with their children, although Beth already knew.

After they finished their light lunch, they packed up the leftovers, put them in the cooler and into the large bag. They had enough time to explore part of the island before Meeko returned to pick them up.

Millie had remembered to bring her cell phone and snapped several selfies of Nic and her and of Scout. She was able to snap some spectacular shots of the turquoise water and the cruise ship, off in the distance.

Scout darted ahead but they easily caught up with him when he stopped to sniff the tips of a nearby bush. "He's going to be all tuckered out by the time we get back."

They stepped off the path to check out a small cove when Scout, who had once again trotted ahead of them, leapt into the air and let out a small yelp.

Millie darted down the trail to see what was wrong and caught a glimpse of a dark green reptile. She stopped in her track. "Agh!"

Nic laughed when he caught up with Scout and Millie. "Ah...it's an iguana. They won't hurt you."

The iguana was almost the same size as the small dog. Scout dashed back to the couple and hopped on top of Millie's sandal. She picked him up and held him to her. "That's what you get for being so curious."

He didn't seem keen on wandering too far ahead after that and all too soon it was time for them to head back to the beach to gather their belongings and wait for the shuttle boat.

Millie nudged Scout into his carrier and closed the door before picking him up.

The small boat appeared on the horizon. It drew closer and they waited near the water's edge as the boat drifted to shore.

Nic handed Scout and his carrier to Meeko followed by the bag of leftover food while Millie waited on the beach. Nic returned a second time for his soon-to-be-wife and reached for her hand as they slowly waded out to the boat.

She cast several wistful glances back at the secluded slice of paradise that had been theirs for a few short hours and then scooted across the bow of the boat.

Nic pushed the boat deeper into the water before he jumped onto the bow and made his way to the bench seat.

Meeko, a St. Croix native, grinned at them as he turned the small boat around, his bright white smile filling his face. "I trust you had a nice visit to our wonderful island."

Nic winked at Meeko. "Yes, we did Meeko. Mission accomplished...she said 'yes.'"

"Tis good to be married." Meeko nodded at Nic and then focused his attention on navigating the vessel but not before he turned the boat's radio on and a soft romantic song began to play.

Millie snuggled close to Nic and closed her eyes as she leaned her head against him. Nothing could ruin the wonderful, magical day. She would cherish it for the rest of her life.

When the boat docked a short time later, Meeko helped Nic unload their belongings before helping Millie climb onto the dock.

"Congratulations," Meeko said.

Nic and Millie thanked him for helping make their day special and they slowly wandered back to the ship. "I fear I must get back to work to prepare for departure."

Millie glanced at her watch. Their time together had flown by. "I'm going to hang around out here and call Beth. I'll see you later."

Nic kissed Millie, a sweet gentle kiss that held so much promise. As he made his way up the gangway, the crew saluted him, welcoming him back. Millie's heart swelled with pride. He was her love...her man.

She stepped off to the side, plucked her phone from her back pocket, switched it on and dialed her daughter's cell phone number.

"Hi Mom." Beth picked up right away.

"Hi Beth." Millie slyly smiled. "Are you finally home?"

"Yeah. We finally made it back. Whew! What a mess. Did you get the pictures I sent to you?"

"Yes. Thank you. They were great pictures. The group photo was a nice one. At least you were able to enjoy part of one day of your cruise.

You'll have to come back and try again," Millie said. "How is your father?"

"Dad is doing okay. We're working on funeral arrangements right now. He hasn't mentioned suing the cruise line today but then I only talked to him briefly," Beth said. "I'm glad to be home."

"I'm sure you are. That's nice of you to help your father with the arrangements."

"I had no choice. Linda and her husband, Mike, got into a huge fight at the hotel right before we left for the airport. The front desk had to call hotel security. We're lucky they didn't call the cops and have both of them arrested."

"The husband should cut Linda some slack. After all, her mother just passed away," Millie said.

"That's what I thought too, but I think there's more to the story. From what I could gather when you could understand what they were shouting at each other, Linda found out Mike had taken some photos of one of the women who worked on board the cruise ship and he admitted he was attracted to her."

Millie loosened her grip on the phone and it started to slip from her grasp. "Oh no! Did you happen to get a name or description?"

"No. I mean it was an all-out brawl. She was hitting him and he was trying to get away from her." Beth paused. "When the hotel security arrived, Mike refused to press charges."

Millie's mind was racing in a million different directions. "What...what does Mike look like?"

He's short, roundish and balding on top," Beth said.

"Dark hair?"

"Yep."

Beth changed the subject. "Did you take the day off?"

Despite the chaotic thoughts rumbling round her head, Millie grinned. Her daughter was fishing, trying to find out if Nic had proposed.

"Yeah," she answered vaguely. "I already had the time scheduled and it's such a beautiful day."

"What did you do?" Beth asked.

"I was going to ask Captain Armati if he had time off but I found out he'd already asked one of the female dancers to join him for lunch," Millie said. "What a jerk."

Beth gasped on the other end. There was a moment of silence and Millie had to clamp her hand tight across her mouth to stop herself from busting out laughing.

"You're kidding!"

"I am."

"You are what?"

"I'm kidding," Millie said. "I'm also engaged to the wonderful man."

"Mom," Beth squealed. "That was not nice."

"I know," Millie agreed. "But it was fun. I had no idea you met him." Nic had invited Beth and her family to dine with him at the captain's table where he hoped to get to know Millie's family, but after Delilah's demise and they got off the ship in San Juan, he hadn't had a chance.

Millie had no idea they'd met. "He admitted he secretly invited you, David and the kids to not only tour the bridge but also visit his apartment which is when he told you what he planned."

"He did," Beth said. "It was so hard to keep it a secret. He's such a nice man and ooh-la-la, that sexy Italian accent and smoldering brown eyes."

Millie turned a shade of pink at her daughter's description of her future husband. "He's wonderful," she simply said. She told her daughter their plan to announce the engagement and then pick a date that would work best for all of the children. "We decided to wed in Miami. It will be easier for Nic's family to come from Italy and an easy direct flight for you from Michigan."

They chatted for a while longer, until Millie realized she needed to get back to work. "Thanks for everything, Beth." What she really meant was thank you to her daughter for supporting her, for supporting her career and approving of Nic.

Millie told her daughter she loved her and to hug her grandchildren for her before she told her good-bye.

She turned off her cell phone and as she headed back to the ship, it dawned on her she had a good idea what had happened to Delilah Osborne and by whom.

Chapter 19

Millie caught up with Andy near the gangway.

"Right on time. I trust you had a nice day."

"I did. I had a wonderful day, one of the best days of my life," she said.

"Oh?" Andy lifted a brow. "Buck Island is beautiful, a wonderful island to escape the crowds but the best day of your life?"

"Yep." Millie nodded.

"Why..." Andy didn't have time to finish his question as a group of sunburned guests approached, asking if the ship sold aloe for sunburns.

"They do," Millie said. "The gift shop, Ocean Treasures, doesn't open until the ship departs St. Croix around five-thirty." She lifted her hand and pointed to the ship's signage near the bank of elevators. "The store is up on deck seven."

The group walked away and Andy grabbed Millie's ring finger. He stared at the diamond engagement ring and his mouth dropped open. "You..."

A slow smile spread across his face and, in a rare display of affection, Andy wrapped his arms around Millie and hugged her tight. "Congratulations Millie. I'm so happy."

Millie blinked back the tears. "Thanks Andy," she choked. "So am I."

"Ahem."

Andy released Millie from the bear hug and she spun around to face Captain Vitale. "I hear congratulations are in order." Captain Vitale embraced Millie. "I've been wondering when this would happen."

Within moments, both crew and passengers surrounded Millie and showered her with heartfelt congratulations.

"This calls for an engagement party." Annette, who had heard through the grapevine from Amit, who had been delivering a late lunch to Captain Vitale in the bridge and overheard the captain telling the staff captain he had just proposed.

Captain Armati and Millie's engagement spread through the ship like wildfire. Millie was a mini celebrity for the rest of the afternoon as the crew, staff and passengers alike stopped to congratulate her. Millie only wished Nic could be there to share in the celebration.

Finally, the last passenger and crewmember boarded the ship. Suharto gave the all clear to pull the gangway and the ship set sail.

"Good afternoon ladies and gentleman. This is Captain Armati speaking to you from the bridge." A thrill ran up Millie's spine as she listened to his voice. "I trust you had a wonderful afternoon on the spectacular island of St. Croix. I would like to personally thank each of you for the sincere congratulations on my engagement to Millie Sanders, Assistant Cruise Director aboard Siren of the Seas."

Millie's face turned three shades of red and Andy patted her shoulder.

The captain finished the announcement by telling them that the following day they would visit the island of St. Thomas and the ship was scheduled to dock around six a.m. with passengers allowed to disembark by seven. After he signed off, well-wishers once again surrounded Millie.

Danielle was one of the last to arrive. She shook her head at Millie. "I figured you would get tired of being my roomie eventually, but do you have to run off and marry the captain just to get away?"

Millie rolled her eyes. "Don't worry. I'm going to personally pick my replacement," she said.

"I don't know if that's a threat or a promise." Danielle gave Millie a quick hug and took a step back. "Let me see the ring."

Millie held out her hand. "Whew! Your ring is gorgeous. Captain Armati is a lucky man."

Danielle glanced at the clock near the elevators. "I better get going. We have a sail away singles Mix and Mingle. If I'm lucky creep-o won't be there."

Danielle's words reminded Millie of her conversation with Beth. "Wait!"

Millie pulled her cell phone from her back pocket, switched it on and pulled up the recent text from her daughter. She flipped through the pictures her daughter had sent until she got to the one of the entire party...Delilah, Roger, Delilah's family as well as Beth and her family.

She tapped the screen to enlarge the photo and turned the phone so Danielle could see. "The guy on the right, does he look familiar?"

Danielle squinted her eyes and studied the photo. Her eyes widened. "That's the guy! How did..." Her voice trailed off. "Oh my gosh! That man was part of your ex's group."

"And I also believe he's Delilah's killer." She told Danielle how Beth had said Linda and her husband had gotten into a huge fight before leaving for the airport. "I need to call Beth."

Millie hurried to the open deck. Danielle was right behind her.

They were not far from the island and Millie's cell phone still had service. She quickly dialed her daughter's number. "Hi Mom. I thought you'd be out to sea by now."

"We're on our way and I only have a minute to talk. I need to ask you, does Delilah have any other children?"

"Let me think." There was a moment of silence. "No. She had a son. From what Dad told me he died in a car accident when he was a teen. There's only Linda."

"Thanks. That's all I wanted to know. I think I know what happened to Delilah but I'll have to wait to confirm my suspicions." She thanked her daughter again before disconnecting the line.

"Delilah wanted to buy my house. She told me Roger and she needed a bigger place because she thought her daughter might be moving in with them. She only has one daughter." Millie began to pace. "Perhaps Delilah was trying to break up Linda's marriage, Mike got angry or scared and he killed Delilah."

"Or Delilah found out about his cheating and confronted him. He panicked and killed her," Danielle theorized.

"Motive and opportunity. Motive was Delilah attempting to convince her daughter to leave her husband. "You called him 'Mark' but he must've lied. His name is Mike. Mike knew about Delilah's allergies, snuck into her cabin and tainted her food."

Danielle wrinkled her nose. "It's a stretch. Sure, he's a creep but it doesn't make him a killer."

There was something else nagging in the back of Millie's mind. Something else tied Mike to Delilah's death. If only she could talk to the Boskos. Perhaps Delilah had confided in them that she feared her son-in-law and asked them to come along for moral support.

The only way she could find out was to ask them, and although she was tempted, she was in no hurry to expose herself to the norovirus. She had just enough time to track down Dave Patterson and share her suspicions.

Millie headed to her cabin to freshen up and change into her work uniform before making a beeline for Patterson's office. For once, he was in his office. He listened quietly as Millie told him all she knew, how a male passenger had subjected Danielle to unwanted advances and they discovered the man was Delilah's son-in-law. She told him about the argument between Linda and Mike at the hotel and how Delilah had told her that her daughter might be moving in with them.

She also told him the Boskos might have more information because the couple had not wanted to come on the cruise in the first place. "They might not know *who* Delilah feared but may have other helpful information."

"I'll get right on it." Patterson congratulated Millie on her engagement and teased her about catching a big fish before walking her to the door. "I ran into Annette upstairs and she's already working on an engagement party and an extravagant dinner menu. Andy is excited too. He's meeting with the orchestra to put together some special music. It sounds like they plan to turn your engagement party into a real blowout."

"It sounds like a lot of fun." Millie reached for the door handle and then froze. "Food. That's it!" Millie spun around. "Sushi!"

"You like sushi?" Patterson asked. "I do too."

"No." Millie shook her head. "I hate sushi. Delilah and the others had been hanging out, listening to live music prior to heading to the dining room for dinner the night she died. Someone in their party had picked up some pre-dinner appetizers at the Appeteasers Snack Bar and one of them had peanut butter."

Millie's heart began to pound. "I would almost bet Mike Foster was the person who offered to bring back the pre-dinner appetizers and he gave one of them to Delilah in his first attempt to poison her."

Patterson appeared doubtful but promised Millie when he spoke to the Boskos he would ask them if they remembered who had gone to Appeteasers.

Millie thanked Patterson for following up and then, with pep in her step, headed upstairs. She was almost certain she'd inadvertently uncovered the killer!

Chapter 20

"Poor Roger," Millie said in a low voice as she and Nic...Captain Armati, hurried toward the theater where an engagement party was about to get underway to celebrate their upcoming nuptials.

"It's a shame things had to end that way," Nic said. "Not only is Roger mourning the loss of Delilah, her family now has to deal with the fact Delilah's son-in-law is a murderer."

Dave Patterson had talked to the Boskos and more clues were uncovered. Delilah had suspected her son-in-law was out to harm her but had not wanted to say anything to her daughter since Linda loved Mike, almost to a fault.

The Boskos had planned to stay on board and speak to the authorities after Mike and the others departed, fearing if he suspected they knew more than they let on, the unstable man would go off the deep end and kill them.

They'd never gotten around to it after succumbing to norovirus and being confined to their room.

Patterson alerted the authorities in Grand Rapids of the information and when they'd questioned Mike Foster, at first he denied it but after several hours of interrogation, had confessed to tainting Delilah's food with a thin layer of peanut paste but swore he only wanted to scare her, not kill her.

"All I can say is I'm glad the black cloud of suspicion is no longer hanging over my head," Millie said.

"Me too, my love." They stopped in front of the double doors leading to the lower level of the theater. Nic reached for the door handle. "We're going to have to work on keeping you out of trouble," he said as he leaned forward and gently kissed her lips.

"But…"

Nic held a finger to her lips. "I'm teasing. Now let's go celebrate!"

The end.

If you enjoyed reading "Suite Revenge," please take a moment to leave a review. It would be greatly appreciated! Thank you!

Cruise Ship Christian Cozy Mysteries Series
Book #9…coming soon!

Get Free Books and More!

Sign up for my Free Cozy Mysteries Newsletter to get free and discounted books, giveaways & soon-to-be-released books!

hopecallaghan.com/newsletter

Meet The Author

Hope Callaghan is an author who loves to write Christian books, especially Christian Mystery and Cozy Mystery books. She has written more than 45 mystery books (and counting) in five series.

Born and raised in a small town in West Michigan, she now lives in Florida with her husband.

She is the proud mother of one daughter and a stepdaughter and stepson. When she's not doing the thing she loves best - writing books - she enjoys cooking, traveling and reading books.

Hope loves to connect with her readers! Connect with her today!

Visit hopecallaghan.com for special offers, free books, and soon-to-be-released books!

Email: hope@hopecallaghan.com

Facebook:
https://www.facebook.com/hopecallaghanauthor/

Chicken Pot Pie Recipe

Ingredients:

1 lb. chicken breasts (bone in)

1 cup sliced carrots

1 cup frozen green peas

1 small diced potato

½ cup celery diced

1 small yellow onion chopped

¼ cup butter

1/3 cup all-purpose flour

2 tsp salt, plus ½ tsp

1 tsp black pepper, plus ¼ tsp

¼ tsp celery seed

1-3/4 cup chicken broth (reserved from stock)

2/3 cup milk

2 – 9 inch unbaked pie crusts

Directions:

Add thawed chicken breasts PLUS 2 tsp salt, 1 tsp pepper to boiling water. Cook for ½ hour (at boiling).

Add carrots, peas, potatoes, onion and celery. Cook for an additional 15 minutes.

Remove from heat, cool. (To speed it up, we removed chicken and placed in a bowl of cold water.

Debone chicken, cut into cubes. Add back to broth/veggie mixture. Mix and heat.
Remove from stove.

Strain juice/broth. Set aside.

*Preheat oven to 425 degrees.
In saucepan over medium heat, melt butter. Stir in flour, ½ tsp salt, ¼ tsp pepper and celery seed. Slowly stir in chicken broth and milk.

Simmer over medium-low heat until thickened. Remove from heat, set aside.

Place piecrust in bottom of ungreased pie pan.

Spread the chicken/veggie mixture in bottom of piecrust.

Pour hot liquid (broth) mixture over top. (If the mixture gets too thick, add extra broth – until "pourable".)

Cover with top crust, seal edges and cut away excess dough. Make several small slits in top to allow steam to escape.

Bake in preheated oven for 30 to 35 minutes or until pastry is golden brown and filling is bubbly. Cool for 10 minutes before serving.
  *We covered the edges of the piecrust with tinfoil so that it wouldn't burn and then removed the tinfoil halfway thru baking.

  *Makes one 9-inch homemade pot pie.

42489607R00184

Made in the USA
San Bernardino, CA
06 December 2016